# TO HER MASTER BORN

by

## MARIA ISABEL PITA

## CHIMERA

To Her Master Born first published in 2002 by
Chimera Publishing Ltd
PO Box 152
Waterlooville
Hants
PO8 9FS

Printed and bound in Great Britain by
Cox & Wyman Ltd, Reading.

The characters and situations in this book are entirely imaginary and bear no relation to any real person or actual happening.

# TO HER MASTER BORN

## Maria Isabel Pita

*To my beautiful Master, Stinger.*


'*...This is the power of fantasy: the natural power of physical growth metamorphosed into a soul force.*'

*Rudolf Steiner*

# Prologue

Juliet is standing before the window, her attention torn between the ominous horizon and the even more desolate face of her mother sitting at the table in the dark room behind her. The *Message* said they were coming for her today, yet the sun is already setting behind the black clouds and she is still here in the miserable little cottage where she grew up.

'Come and sit down, Juliet.' Her mother's weather-beaten face falls into her callused hands. 'Please, sweetheart.'

'But what if they do not come, mum?'

'Oh they will *come* all right.'

Juliet feels only reassured by the grim statement, but looking eagerly out the window again, she still sees no sign of life on the packed-dirt road.

'Nothing is easy in life,' her mother warns. 'Those of us who are not noble-born must work for our living, all of us, including you, Juliet, whether you like it or not.'

'Oh mum, stop it!' She has been enduring this kind of talk since the sun came up. It was easy to ignore in the morning when she felt nothing but excited, but now fear of disappointment is sharpening the words' power to affect her. 'Just because you had a miserable life, mum, does not mean I have to.' She fights back with anger. 'I cannot possibly settle—'

She stops talking as abruptly as if a hand falls over her mouth to silence her, because she can scarcely believe what she finally sees appear on the horizon. 'Oh my God,' she whispers.

'You can still change your mind, Juliet, it is not too late,' her mother begs. 'You cannot believe what they tell you, it is not true!'

Her daughter promptly opens the front door and runs outside. She is afraid what she sees might only be an illusion, merely three low-flying ravens, but it really *is* three black-clad riders on black horses. Suddenly she cannot be sure if the faint sound of thunder she hears is coming from the sky or from the road, where twelve hooves are beating against the packed earth at full gallop. All the long day she was afraid they would not come and expected to feel only joy in this moment, instead her apprehension intensifies when it dawns on her that *she* is the sole reason for this exercise of power and speed heading directly towards her.

Her right hand falls unconsciously over her bosom, half swelling out of a black bodice she laced up as tightly as possible over a low-cut white shirt with long sleeves. Her ankle-length skirt is also black, and all she is wearing beneath it are her worn leather shoes, which do not match the incredibly fine white stockings that came with the *Message* along with a mysterious length of white lace. It took her some time to understand the latter was a belt to be worn around her waist, from which dangle four shorter pieces of cloth ending in little metal clasps to hold up the stockings. She had never seen anything like it before in all her nineteen years on earth.

Thank God her father is still out in the fields this evening. Naturally, her mother told him about the *Message* when it arrived, but he said absolutely nothing about it. He simply sat down at the table as usual, ripped into his bread, dunked the fragrant dough into his hot beef stew, and chewed doggedly staring into space. Since that moment he avoided his daughter's eyes as though she had ceased to exist for him.

There is no doubt about the fact now that the deep rumbling sound she hears is coming from the three men on horseback and not from the sky. She says a quick prayer of thanks beneath her breath it is not raining, which would ruin her appearance. Her mother brushed her long blonde hair until it shone and individual strands wafted up into the air crackling against the brush. Now she needlessly pinches some color into her cheeks, already attractively flushed with emotion, and holds her back straight and proud.

All three riders are wearing long black capes she can hear snapping in the wind over the growing roar of the horses' hooves, the only two sounds in the world on this strangely still and overcast evening. All the chickens usually clucking noisily around the yard have taken refuge inside the coop to avoid the coming storm, except for one small hen standing perfectly still facing the trees, the direction from which wolves come…

Juliet quickly crosses herself, praying for courage to keep all her wits about her, because without them she is worthless. Lord Wulvedon will not look at her twice if he senses nothing but an ignorant country girl trembling in awe before him. She must prove to him *she* is the one he has been searching for; that *she* is the one he scours the countryside for every autumn while lesser men harvest their crops. Even though Juliet knows she is only one of a dozen maidens who received the *Message* on the last full moon in September, she also knows she is special, she *has* to be.

The first rider rears his horse to a stop so close to her it takes all her willpower not to back away from him timidly. His companions pull up just behind him, the long capes she mistook for black wings from a distance settling softly around them. Lord Wulvedon is not with them, of course, these are only his messengers.

She stares bravely up at the leader even though she feels faint from the sudden overwhelming smell of horse sweat mingled with leather, a powerful combination intensified by the charged stillness of the atmosphere. He tosses his cape over one shoulder as he grasps the reins tightly in one hand and trots even closer to her, until he is looming directly above her and his leg is nearly brushing her arm. She has to throw her head back to keep her eyes on his face, but it is nearly impossible to make out his features in the overcast dusk.

'Juliet,' he says quietly.

'Yes…' She has to swallow all the conflicting emotions crowding in her throat. 'Yes, my lord.' She has never before seen a man dressed entirely in black. The beautiful horse's neck gleams with sweat, and the material of its rider's vest and leggings shine in a similar fashion, but coolly, without strain.

'You are prepared to leave your home and come with us, Juliet, bringing with you only the clothes on your back?'

His deep voice helps steady her nerves. 'Yes, my lord.'

'Then raise your skirt.'

She becomes aware of her heart beating against her breast, the only part of her that can seem to move.

'Do not make me ask you again, Juliet. We need to make sure you have done as you were instructed.'

The fact that he is kind enough to tell her the reason for his shocking request reassures her somewhat, giving her hands the strength they need to grasp her skirt, and pull it slowly up to her knees.

'All the way, Juliet.' His tone is slightly harder now, as if he is growing impatient.

She glances over her shoulder at the cottage where she will be condemned to remain if she does not take hold of her courage now before it is too late… before they turn their horses around and leave her there in the grass with the chickens where she will have proved she belongs…

She quickly raises her skirt as far as she can, gathering its full folds against her swiftly beating heart. The cool evening air caresses the naked tops of her thighs and her flat belly, but she is really only aware of the mysteriously hot touch of the men's eyes on her most private parts.

'Are you a virgin, Juliet?'

She stares at his black boot thrust firmly into the stirrup as she replies softly, 'Yes, my lord.'

'Well, we will see.'

His cool skepticism brings a furious color to her cheeks, and yet she can hardly blame him for doubting her virtue when she is standing there like that.

'You may lower you skirt now.'

She lets it fall protectively around her again, even as she wonders at the curiously warm feeling between her thighs, which makes no sense at all in the chilly twilight.

'Are you having second thoughts, Juliet?'

She stares fixedly at the horizon where lightning has begun to flash like a reflection of the novel sensations in her belly. 'No, my lord…'

'This is your last chance to say no, Juliet. From now on the word no and the freedom of choice that attends it will cease to exist for you. Do you understand?'

'Yes, my lord, I understand.'

One of the other men dismounts abruptly, and she somehow manages not to immediately condemn herself as a liar by running away as he approaches her. It is almost a relief when he grabs her by the waist and she feels the silent statements of his fingers telling her it is too late; she no longer has a choice. 'Raise your skirt again,' he commands quietly, 'you are riding like a man tonight.'

This time she obeys at once, and he lifts her effortlessly while the man in charge slips an arm beneath her leg to help it across the saddle behind him. His cloak makes it impossible for her to slip her arms around his chest and hold on to him. All she can do is clutch the rim of the saddle behind her as he turns his restless beast around sharply and gallops down the road towards the lightning. It takes all her concentration to hold on and not be thrown. The muscles in her calves cling desperately to the horse's hot, slick belly even as she becomes increasingly aware of the most vulnerable part of her – the totally sensitive space between her thighs – rubbing up against the man holding the reins as he flies bravely through the darkness with her. He is so hard against her, and the motion is so relentless, a sensation such as she has never known gradually begins dawning inside her. Soon the feeling is all she is aware of because it is making her so weak and breathless she is afraid of losing her grip on the saddle.

'Oh, my lord,' she cries, 'please, stop!' She is sure he heard her even over the deafening rush of the wind and the thunder of hooves, but he does not stop, and for a few blinding, stunning moments her body completely forgets her fear.

# Chapter One

Isabella gladly accepts the hand the driver offers her so she can step gracefully out of the carriage. His strong, black-gloved fingers swallow her delicate ones, and squeeze them to help brace her as she sways weakly on her feet. She has been sitting in a shaking and enclosed space for so long, solid ground and fresh air come as a breathtaking shock.

'Thank you,' she says, her golden-brown eyes on a level with his chest, which strikes her a reassuringly familiar extension of the carriage's black interior.

'Will you be all right, miss?'

Her dark-lashed eyes, large and shining from countless days of staring out at rolling hills and the dark edges of forests, alight on his hard mouth. 'Yes, thank you,' she repeats firmly even as her pulse flutters like a baby bird clinging to a branch, terrified of flying into the world on its own. But she has no choice now the warm safe nest of her father's love is gone forever.

The lines in his weathered face take on the appearance of grim statements, and he seems about to tell her something, yet all he says is, 'Good luck to you then, miss.' He turns back to the horses, his only real concern; passengers come and go.

The black trunk with time-rusted hinges containing all her worldly possessions sits like an unnaturally perfect rock on the immaculate lawn. It looked so big to her in her small bedroom when she was packing it, smoothing her garments down with her hands and her emotions with her thoughts as she told herself over and over again this was a position she could not afford to pass up. Penniless orphans and young respectable females with no dowry have to take whatever work they can get, wherever they can find it. Fortunately her father, who raised her all by himself after her mother died giving birth to her, saw to her education. He had not done so for any practical reasons, God bless him, but because he valued learning above all else, and his bright, beautiful daughter was the vessel into which he poured all his knowledge of history and science, language and culture. Isabella's trunk is stuffed to bursting with clothes and books, and her mind is equally full of all the information her father packed into it until the night he died.

She feared the locks on her trunk would snap open during the long and often bumpy journey, but they held fast, so at least all her dresses and shoes, and the journals she has kept since she was a little girl, are not strewn across the countryside. For whatever it is worth, her personality is still intact. However, the gray stone building looming behind her trunk now makes it look as small as a child's box, disturbingly insignificant in the vast and powerful scheme of things.

'You are sure they are expecting you, miss?'

She looks back at the driver where he is perched in his high seat again with the reins in his hands, ready to leave her there alone. 'They should be…' She does not mean to sound uncertain, but his attitude is making her nervous. Even his four brown horses, which have already traveled countless miles today already, are shifting restively, as if eager to be on the move again before nightfall. 'This *is* the Wulvedon Estate, is it not?'

He glances up at the sprawling array of sharp black rooftops, delicate spires and thick towers. 'It is.' He turns his head away from her and spits.

Sincerely hoping it was accumulated dust from the road and not something else that prompted his rude gesture, she lifts her long black skirt and steps quickly away from the carriage. The large wheels whisper across the grass as he turns the horses back towards the road, and the thunder of hooves fills her head, trampling all her thoughts as she watches the beautiful muscular bodies galloping away. Then a profound silence envelops her and she wraps it around herself for a lovely moment, free of anxiety's bitter cold to simply enjoy the dying light flowing across the grass like liquid gold. Every blade shines like an emerald and makes all her worries seem worthlessly foolish, because deep inside she knows everything will be all right, that everything will be much more than just all right, if she does not lose heart.

She turns back towards her forbidding new home, and abruptly catches sight of a man's tall and lean figure silhouetted against the setting sun. He is walking towards the Castle with long, relaxed strides, two large dogs following eagerly at his heels. He is too far away to hear her should she call out to him, but that is not why she refrains from trying to get his attention. The way he carries himself, his aura of restrained power outlined for her by the glowing horizon, tells her he is a nobleman and not a servant she can ask to help with her trunk. Then he disappears into the stone wall surrounding the Castle as though she only imagined him.

Isabella does not move until the door closes, and even then all she does is turn her head from side to side unable to believe what she sees. Part of her expects the floor to start shaking beneath her feet, thereby proving she has dozed off in the carriage and is only dreaming she arrived at her destination.

She raises her skirt slightly and looks down at the tips of her boots – small black pyramids on a green field – for the entire floor is covered by a rug that seems to have captured her journey. Rolling hills and dark forests are woven into it with a flat, child-like simplicity, the legs of wooden furniture rising like tree trunks giving it a haunting sense of dimension. She has never seen anything like it before in all her twenty-three years. Obviously, this feeling of nervous awe is something she is going to have to get used to. She spent most of her life happily cooped up with her father in his library. Whenever she left their little townhouse she followed a well-worn path between the market and the bookstore happily believing she had all she needed to nourish body and soul. She has been on the Wulvedon estate for less than one hour, however, and already she is distressed to realize just how poor she actually is. She could not have conceived of anything lovelier than the glow of firelight on the gilded leather spines of old books, yet now her cherished memory of home feels like only one golden-brown leaf in a vast forest of unimaginable beauty.

As if gradually being released from a spell, Isabella turns her whole body around slowly, still taking in her lavish surroundings.

She has read about such wealth, but she would not have thought a mere governess would be given such a room. Yet judging by all the long dark corridors she walked down to get here, the Castle is full of such spacious chambers. For all she knows this is one of the smallest and plainest. Large mirrors set in frames of elaborately carved wood hang on every high wall, and she catches sight of herself from every direction as she turns like a little ballerina in a music box, her back tense with wonder.

It was always too dark for her to see her face clearly in the small looking-glass she kept in her bedroom, the only thing she inherited from her mother, but so many candles are burning in this windowless room that it is bright as day. She is surrounded by a small fortune in wax alone, and the white-and-lavender canopy bed is bigger than the carriage that brought her here. She approaches it slowly, strangely conscious of the sound of her breathing rising above the fervent crackling of wicks. She can scarcely believe that every night from now on she is going to sleep on a luxuriously elevated surface she will have to climb three steps to reach.

A quick, light knock on the door interrupts her progress towards the dream-like bed. She turns back to face the carved oak surface wondering what the old servant who escorted her here forgot to tell her. Perhaps she brought her to the wrong room? Isabella sincerely hopes not, for her emotions have already begun to take root here…

'May I come in?' A woman's cheerful voice penetrates the thick wood.

'Yes…' Isabella calls back uncertainly.

The door opens.

Her breath catches as an emotion she has never experienced before hatches in her heart, causing her to glance self-consciously down at her black homespun dress as she abruptly realizes how terribly plain it is.

Her visitor pushes closed, and locks, the heavy door behind her before she turns, leans against it with her hands behind her back, and smiles.

The crackling of hundreds of wicks seems unnaturally loud as the two young women stare silently across the room at each other.

Finally, Isabella remembers herself. 'Good evening, mistress,' she says, oddly conscious of the words shaping themselves on her tongue.

'Good evening.' The lady's smile broadens as she pushes herself away from the door and walks deeper into the room.

Isabella is entranced by the gleam of candlelight in her visitor's long sage-green skirt. She has of course read about materials like silk and satin, but she has never actually seen them on a person in such luxurious abundance, only in bookmarks or as a runner on the altar at church. The bodice is made of the same rich material as the skirt, only it is rust-colored and held up as if by magic, since it is sleeveless and strapless.

The vision stops a body's length away from her and opens her slender arms wide. 'How do you like your room?'

Isabella's answer is delayed by an enthralled contemplation of her visitor's belt, which is woven to look like a vine blooming with large, rust-colored flowers encircling her narrow hips. 'It is too beautiful for words, mistress,' she answers truthfully.

The woman laughs, a pleasantly light, cascading flow of sound. 'My name is Bridget, and I see you like my gown, too.'

'Oh yes…'

Bridget turns around slowly, gracefully showing herself off. 'I have hundreds of dresses,' she declares proudly. Her pale skin is flawless and her golden-brown hair has been artfully harvested up off her bare shoulders with pearl-tipped pins. There is no telling just how far down her back it will fall when let loose, but Isabella can tell it would be smooth and soft and shining and lovelier than anything else in the room. That strange new feeling takes deeper root in her heart as she tries not to look directly at Bridget's full breasts swelling dangerously inside the tight, heart-shaped bodice. They seem at odds with her fine bone structure and keep irresistibly drawing her eyes down towards them.

'It is all right.' Bridget slips her hands behind her back again, thrusting out her bosom. 'You may look. I do not mind.'

Isabella feels a confused blush warm her own creamy cheeks.

Bridget laughs again happily, rushes towards her, and flings her arms around her. 'Oh, I am going to like you!' she whispers.

Isabella is overwhelmed by a world of novel sensations – cool, stiff and silky, warm, tender and yet also strong.

Bridget steps back. 'You poor thing.' She gazes searchingly down into Isabella's face with her dark-green eyes. 'You are an orphan, I know.'

Isabella hangs her head.

'Well, do not be sad. I will be taking good care of you from now on, my dear... I will be sure not to let my brother see you.'

Isabella channels all her anxious awe and confusion into the question. 'Your brother?'

'My identical twin brother, although his hair is dark.' She catches a stray wisp of Isabella's hair between two fingertips, crowned by long nails painted to match her bodice. 'As dark as yours.'

Isabella looks away shyly, unable to imagine a man as handsome as Bridget is beautiful.

'But what am I thinking?' her hostess asks cheerfully. 'You must be anxious to wash up after your long journey. Here, let me help you out of this dreadful garment you are hiding in.'

Isabella slinks out of her reach, shocked by the mere suggestion of undressing in front of anyone.

Bridget's eyes sparkle above her smile, which also matches her bodice. 'You are a shy little pussy, are you not?'

She does not know what to say to this, so she asks, 'When do I meet the little girl I will be instructing?'

Bridget takes her firmly by the shoulders, and turns her around. 'Let us get this off you so I can have it burned at once!'

Isabella's thoughts stumble all over each other and her racing heart does not help her confusion. So far, her new position is nothing like she imagined it would be. 'But this is one of my best dresses,' she protests, possessed by the strange feeling she has ended up in the wrong play, because none of the polite lines she rehearsed in the carriage seem to fit.

'Nonsense.' Bridget is making quick work of all the tiny hooks running down the length of Isabella's back. 'I intend to have a whole new wardrobe made for you.'

'But…' She is about to say she cannot possibly afford to pay for new dresses but stops herself, afraid of insulting her hostess by doubting her generosity.

'But *what*, Isabella? I have to look at you every day, and you look like a skinny little crow. After a fortnight of proper meals, and a few visits from my seamstress, you will hardly recognize yourself.'

Her head spinning, Isabella decides to concentrate on one question at a time. 'You will be sitting in on the classes?'

Bridget turns her around to face her again. 'Of course, silly, how else am I to learn? We will be teaching each other.' She peels the black cloth away from Isabella's chest and pulls the long sleeves down her arms quickly, carelessly turning the garment inside out. 'And the first thing you need to learn, my little stray kitten, is never to assume anything. How can you tolerate such a cheap, rough material against your skin?' A frown replaces her smile as she contemplates Isabella's white slip, which covers every inch of her body. 'Oh, just take it all off,' she says in disgust, turning away, 'and come over here.'

'But—'

'For someone who claims to know four languages you are certainly fond of that one little word, Isabella.' She walks over to a small table upon which sit a large white porcelain jar and bowl, both exquisitely decorated by a design of delicate green vines sprouting tiny blue flowers. 'I said come here, my shy little pussy.'

Isabella bites her lip in order not to say 'but' again. 'What have I assumed, my lady?' She sticks doggedly to her growing trail of questions, afraid of losing her way as she slips out of the heavy black dress.

'You assumed it was a child you would be teaching, but nowhere in the advertisement my brother placed did it say his ward was a little girl.' Bridget raises the heavy pitcher with both hands and begins pouring water into the basin.

'*You* are his ward?' Isabella cannot conceal her amazement, even though she is afraid it might be rude.

'Naturally, he is my older brother, by approximately three minutes. Therefore, until I marry, Lord Wulvedon is my lord and protector. However,' she sets the pitcher back down, 'I never intend to marry.'

Isabella leaps over a few other questions to ask curiously, 'Why do you never wish to marry?'

Smiling mischievously, Bridget crooks a finger at her. 'Come here.'

Isabella finds herself walking towards her without thinking about it, which is quite strange since she usually gives everything she does a great deal of thought.

Bridget suddenly looks stern. 'I believe I told you to take that off, Isabella.'

She stops in her tracks, arrested by the sight of Lady Wulvedon's face, which is so lovely it makes her think of the old frescoes in church, except her expression is all wrong, arrogant and sharp as opposed to gentle and humble; the rather insipid look invariably worn by saints. 'I have never…' Her throat is suddenly so tight she cannot get the words out.

'It is all right, Isabella, sisters undress in front of each other all the time. Is there something about your body you are ashamed of?'

'No.'

Bridget's lips bloom in a smile again. 'You answered that quickly and firmly. Very good.'

Isabella does not understand why she feels herself blushing again.

'Would it make it easier for you,' she slips her arms behind her back, 'if I joined you?'

Isabella quickly looks away as the rust-colored bodice opens up like a butterfly taking flight for a second before expiring across a green velvet chair.

'Now it is your turn, Isabella.'

She has lost the trail of her questions and is deep in a forest of emotions completely in the dark. She has no hope of finding her way out if she does not wish to jeopardize her position here, which she cannot afford to do. She spent the little money her father left her to pay for the journey. She needs to work at least three moons before she can afford a ticket back to the city, where she has nothing, and no one, waiting for her anyway.

'Isabella?'

She bends down, grasps the hem of her slip, and quickly pulls the long garment off over her head.

'That was not so hard, was it?' Bridget's friendly tone is back. 'Now come here and we will wash up together.'

Her eyes averted, Isabella drops the slip and walks towards her obediently. It is a relief to be out of her traveling clothes, which seemed to grow heavier with every mile. It would be chilly in the room if it was not for all the burning candles – hundreds of warm caresses she can feel all over her naked body now.

'Do not tell me you are afraid of water, too,' Bridget teases. 'If you are, we can always pretend to be cats and lick each other clean. I do not have anything you do not have,' she adds more seriously. 'You will not turn to stone if you look at me.'

Oddly enough, Isabella finds this remark reassuring. She has seen a woman's bare breasts in paintings, of course, but it is very different to have a real pair before her not fashioned of canvas and oils but of living flesh and blood.

Bridget arches her back and thrusts her bosom out towards her again. 'Do you like them?'

She finds the question astonishing. 'What is there *not* to like about them?'

'Oh I *am* going to like you!' Bridget claps her hands in delight, and then lets her arms fall to her sides again. 'Would you like to touch them?' she asks soberly.

'Yes…' She is actually curious to know what they feel like. Her own breasts are not as full and Bridget's aureoles are slightly darker than hers, and larger, but a quick glance down tells Isabella the other girl's nipples are not as long and pronounced as hers.

'Then you will have to let me touch *yours*, Isabella.'

'All right.' The request only seems fair, rather like being at the market and exchanging one fruit for another.

'Mm, well then, come closer, my curious little pussy.'

Isabella does not hesitate to reach out and rest both her hands lightly over Lady Wulvedon's breasts. Bridget tosses her head back, sighing, and then cups Isabella's delicate orbs in her own cool hands, gently bouncing and weighing them. 'They are lovely, my dear, perfectly round and firm.'

'I like yours,' she returns the compliment.

'Would you like to know how they feel against your lips, Isabella?'

'Yes,' she whispers, still trying to think of the tender mounds of flesh as innocent fruit, even though she suspects there is something wrong with this logic.

'Then you will have to ask my permission to touch them.'

She hesitates, but she is feeling strangely hungry, and if a few words will buy her something she has never tasted before, something that looks and feels so good... 'May I kiss your breasts, mistress?'

'Yes, you may, Isabella.'

Holding the heavy orbs reverently, she bends and shyly kisses the deep space between them.

'Mm, that was very sweet, Isabella. You may kiss them again.'

She does so at once, this time daring to brush her lips over one of the firm nipples. She did not mean to slip it into her mouth, but Bridget's hands suddenly cupped her head and planted it firmly between her lips. Isabella is astonished to find herself blindly suckling it just like a baby, and is strangely pleased by how much Lady Wulvedon seems to enjoy it. Without being told to, she transfers her curious tongue's attention to Bridget's other nipple, which is firm and tender all at once in a curiously gratifying way.

'Oh Isabella, you wicked little thing...'

She straightens up self-consciously, strangely reluctant

to empty her mouth of the delicious fullness.

Bridget grabs a small lavender washcloth off the table, dips it into the basin of water, and rings it out over Isabella's breasts.

'Oh!' she cries, stumbling backwards, for the water is painfully cold.

Bridget laughs and dips the cloth in the water again. 'Now, now, before we play you have to get clean. Come here and turn around.'

Isabella obeys, but shivers uncontrollably as the frigid water flows down her spine. Then she stumbles forward as Bridget begins scrubbing her back vigorously with the wet cloth.

'Stand still, Isabella!'

She freezes beneath the imperious tone.

Lady Wulvedon steps around her and starts giving the front of her body the same treatment. She then dips the cloth in the water again and squeezes it out over Isabella's head, forcing her to close her eyes as her face is scrubbed clean.

'Now for your legs. You can wash your own feet later. I like seeing you in those little black boots and nothing else.'

The rug beneath their feet darkens as Bridget quickly and efficiently continues to baptize her with the shockingly icy water, until she is clutching her arms and trembling, even more grateful now for the warm licks of the candle flames.

'And now for the most important part of all.' Lady Wulvedon grabs a fresh cloth from the table, dips it in the water, and thrusts it between Isabella's thighs.

She moans and closes her eyes, suddenly acutely aware of a part of her body she never thinks about except as something she has to wipe clean after urinating and as a terrible nuisance during her monthly cycle. But she discovers when someone's hand is working between her legs that it makes her body's secret lips feel very different, as though they have something very important to tell her if she only cares to listen…

'There,' Bridget sounds satisfied, 'now we are ready to play. Let your hair down at once. Take the pins out, unbraid it, and shake it loose.' She tosses the washcloth onto the table, and seats herself in the burgundy velvet chair beside it. 'Come and stand before me while you do it,' she adds, her back straight and her hands lightly grasping the arms of the chair as though she is sitting on a throne.

Isabella stares down at the lion's paws and legs rising alongside Lady Wulvedon's shining green skirt as she removes her two large, strategically placed hairpins. Not sure what to do with them, she lets them fall to the rug and unweaves her braid, tentatively shaking her dark hair out over her shoulders.

Lady Wulvedon looks her up and down slowly. 'Mm…' She smiles. 'Mm!'

Isabella glances down at her body. All she can see are her breasts, which are as perky as if she just stepped in from the cold, and the tips of her black boots.

'Listen to me very carefully, Isabella. You are not to leave your room. Do you understand me?'

This, at least, makes sense; as a servant she does not expect to have the freedom to go wherever she pleases. 'Yes, mistress.'

'The only time you are to leave your room is when my man comes for you so we can have our lessons. Do not worry, I will not keep you cooped up inside all the time; I will often have you instruct me outdoors. You simply are not permitted to go anywhere by yourself. Do I make myself perfectly clear?'

'Yes, mistress.'

'Good, because I cannot take care of you if you disobey me. Now come here, my hungry little pussy.' She lifts her skirt, revealing the black ankle boots and rust-colored stockings she is wearing beneath it. She gathers the rich material up into her lap, exposing soft white flesh above the stockings and a deep shadow between them. 'That is far enough, Isabella, now crawl the rest of the way towards me.'

'I beg your pardon?'

'You heard me, Isabella. Get on all fours like the starving pussy you are and crawl towards me. I have a very special treat waiting for you.'

A shadow falls over her mind, obscuring her thoughts as the mist of total confusion gives her feelings strange and unrecognizable shapes. She should be offended by the humiliating command, yet for some reason she is not. She sinks to her knees and falls forward onto her hands, thinking she will never dare to assume anything again. Then she flings her hair back and gazes up at Lady Wulvedon's sternly beautiful face as she crawls towards her. She suffers a fleeting image of her late father looking down from heaven and seeing her like this, but quickly suppresses it in favor of wondering what the special treat is waiting for her.

Bridget pulls her skirt all the way up to her waist and spreads her legs wide, exposing the creamy insides of her thighs and a neatly trimmed bush almost the same color as her stockings. 'Did you enjoy kissing my breasts and sucking on my nipples, Isabella?'

'Yes, mistress,' she admits.

'Then I believe you will enjoy the very special gift I am going to give you now.'

Her head starts spinning, trying to imagine what this gift might be.

Lady Wulvedon slides her hips forward in the chair so the candlelight falls on the glistening red lips pouting open beneath her softly burning bush. Isabella thinks of turning her face away as they draw nearer, but thinking about it is not doing it, and before she knows it Bridget's voiceless mouth is gently kissing the lips on her face. She grimaces slightly at how wet they are, but they smell so good that she willingly kisses them back.

Bridget grabs her firmly by the hair with both hands, and Isabella is stunned to find her face where it has not been since the moment she slipped out of her mother's womb. She struggles instinctively to pull away from the lips devouring her features, but the rich feast suddenly filling her mouth smells delicious and streams an oddly intoxicating juice onto her tongue… she stops trying to escape and begins lapping up the mysteriously rich cream being offered her, tentatively at first, and then more boldly and more hungrily as it flows more and more generously from the hot core of Lady Wulvedon's flesh. Moaning, she shifts her hips even lower in the chair, and Isabella abruptly discovers what feels like a small, hard seed slip between her curious lips. She traps it gently between her teeth, and then uses the tip of her tongue to play with it, intrigued by the way it responds to her teasing attention by growing thick and juicy as a grape while she savors the surprisingly heady bouquet of Bridget's moans.

'Oh Isabella,' she gasps, 'you are such a good little licker!'

She is learning that she can use her tongue in a whole new way to passionately express without words what she does not understand and never even knew she could feel.

'Oh… oh *yes!*' Bridget clamps her thighs around her head, submerging Isabella's face in her dark loins.

When she is at last released, Isabella gasps for breath and falls back across the rug, strands of hair plastered against her wet lips and cheeks.

'Mm…' Smiling, Bridget kicks her gently out of the way as she rises and lets her skirt fall around her legs again. Utterly dazed, she sits up and watches her new mistress hook her bodice back on with accustomed ease.

'Thank you, Isabella, that was lovely. Now wash your face and put on some clothes. My man will be arriving shortly with a tray of food and a jug of wine.' She does not look back as she adds, 'Remember, do not leave this room. I cannot be responsible for what happens to you if you do.'

# Chapter Two

Despite how comfortable her new bed is, or perhaps because of it, Isabella tosses and turns all night in the grip of vivid dreams she can remember only for a few breathless seconds after she surfaces from a shallow and troubled sleep. Then all the beautiful images flow away like a royal entourage returning to the magical realm from which it came and leaving her alone in her poor little brain again.

It took her forever to extinguish all the candles except one before she climbed up onto her bed with it, careful not to singe the delicate lavender veils flowing around her as she placed the holder inside a niche in the headboard. Then she crawled back to the middle of the mattress and sat back on her heels feeling like a small, helpless creature come upon a much larger predator's den.

As she wolfed down the food delivered to her room by Lady Wulvedon's old male servant, and swallowed the red wine accompanying it like water, she succeeded in not thinking about what had happened. It did not prove too difficult since she had no idea what *had* happened. One minute she was curiously touching her beautiful mistress's breasts, and the next she was eating her alive very much like a wild animal. Fortunately, Bridget seemed to enjoy her savage behavior and afterwards did not appear to think any less of her for it, which is a small comfort now. But it does not relieve her of the burden of trying to understand why she behaved as she did and, even more disturbingly important, why she enjoyed it so much that she completely forgot herself for a few thoughtlessly barbaric moments.

Lying awake in the dark on a narrow bank between one tumultuous dream and the next, Isabella finds herself unable to stop thinking about the hauntingly delicious lips secreted away between Lady Wulvedon's milky thighs. She is no closer to understanding, however, why she responded as she did to their passionately wet and profoundly greedy kiss. In fact, thinking about it is only making her hungry again in that strange way which has nothing to do with food. She should be planning tomorrow's lesson, but she cannot concentrate on it with her head still mysteriously trapped between Bridget's legs.

She shifts restlessly in her white nightgown and tosses yet another pillow away from her. She blew out the last candle before she went to sleep, and she is grateful for the heavy feather comforter since it is quite cold in the room now that all the flames have been snuffed out.

She crosses her hands over her chest and attempts to pray, but she cannot get past whispering '*Our Father who art in heaven.*' Because it is *her* father who is in heaven now and who saw how indecently she behaved this evening. Yet she only did as Lady Wulvedon instructed her to, and her new mistress did not seem at all surprised or distressed by her behavior, on the contrary. So perhaps the best thing to do is to try and forget the incident, to file it away as of one of the many strange dreams she had on this endless night. Yet how can she forget something when it is all she can think about?

Isabella finally wakes up for good, so deep on the first floor of the sprawling Castle no windows break up the room's high walls, only large mirrors reflecting its opulent landscape or absolute darkness, depending on whether or not the candles are lit, which this morning they are not. At least she assumes it is morning, but whatever time it is, she decides to get up anyway. She needs to plan today's lesson, to select the texts and write out the questions she will ask at the end to determine how much she succeeded in teaching her student. She is eager to see the library. Judging by the Castle's monstrous scale, it should be as large as she dreamed it would be. Selling most of her father's books after he died was the hardest thing she ever had to do. Disposing of his few personal possessions made her cry, but it was nothing compared to how she felt giving away his soul little by little for the proverbial three pieces of silver.

Wide awake at the thought of having access to a potentially vast library, she flings off the heavy coverlet and gropes carefully on the headboard's ledge for the box of matches she placed there last night beside the candle. Trembling in the cold nest of the luxurious bed, she flicks her wrist and brings one of the long wooden sticks to life. The flame startles her with its brilliance and beauty – a spark let off by the vivid dreams burning inside her all night, like a fire she kept waking up and putting out with the cold water of her rational mind.

Isabella lights the wick and crawls carefully over to the edge of the soft mattress with the small brass holder in one hand. She walks down the steps onto the rug, and begins lighting the candles on the walls and the lamps on the tables, wondering at how effortlessly and generously the sun floods the world with light. She read somewhere that all the stars flickering like burning wicks in the night sky are also unimaginably distant suns, but she finds this hard to believe as she lights one weakly sputtering wax column after another. She is going to miss having windows she can open to let in fresh air and light, yet it does not seem very grateful of her to feel imprisoned considering how luxurious her accommodations are.

She has barely finished lighting half the room when there is a quiet knock on the door. She quickly puts down the candle she was using to revive the others, and runs to open it.

Lady Wulvedon's old male servant is standing out in the corridor holding a tray heavy with her breakfast.

'Good morning, Ludly.' She smiles and holds the door open for him.

'Good morning, miss.' He enters the room and sets his burden down on a nearby table. He then picks up the tray containing the scant remains of last night's dinner. She was starving after her long journey, and she has always had a hearty appetite.

Isabella continues holding the door open for him as she smiles him out. She tried talking to him yesterday, but the more breathless questions she asked – she cannot even remember what they were now she was in such a state of agitation after Lady Wulvedon left – the more his wrinkled old face seemed to turn to stone. Clearly no information about their employers is going to be forthcoming from Ludly.

Breakfast turns out to be nearly as abundant and just as delicious as dinner. It consists of thick slices of freshly baked bread accompanied by small porcelain vials of strawberry and blueberry preserves, a generous dollop of butter, a large clay glass of milk still warm from the cow, six thick slices of bacon and at least four eggs scrambled with tomatoes, green onions and goat cheese.

'Mm…' she moans, drinking half the glass of milk in one long and thirsty swallow. She devours her repast while speculating about how much time she has before Ludly returns to take her to Lady Wulvedon, or before Bridget shows up on her own. There are no clocks in the room. The only timepiece she could find last night was a large hourglass made of black metal filled with golden sand.

Wiping her mouth and fingers clean with a green cloth napkin, she goes and turns the heavy hourglass over. She cannot assume anything, but perhaps the same amount of time will pass every morning between Ludly bringing her breakfast and returning to take her to Lady Wulvedon. She then sifts through a pile of garments she draped over a chair last night in order to fish her nightgown out of the trunk. She cannot decide which one to wear, recalling Bridget's promise of a whole new wardrobe. She had not realized before just how terribly plain, and how boringly similar in style, all her dresses are. Technically, she is still in mourning for her father, but she is sure he would not mind if she wore her bone-colored dress today with buttons down the front, its severity relieved by a white lace collar.

She throws off her nightgown and is about to slip into the dress when she catches sight of herself in several mirrors at once. She is not accustomed to seeing her body at all, much less from every conceivable angle. She has been trying to ignore the mirrors, but it is hard to do since they are everywhere, and seeing her naked form now unexpectedly, Isabella suffers the unsettling impression that she does not know herself nearly as well as she thought she did. She drops the dress, and approaches the largest mirror.

She walks towards it slowly, fighting its pull as though it is dangerously deep, clear water she is afraid of drowning in. Yet she is curious to see what Lady Wulvedon saw yesterday when she made her undress before her.

Her breasts *are* lovely, cool round balls of dough she kneads tentatively with both hands as she studies them in

32

the glass. They are much more than flour mixed with water, however. They are the mystery of flesh coating her bones mixed with her blood's unique vintage. Her teats are heavy and tender and her nipples have risen in the cold room to the point where it almost aches how firm they are. Her bosom was designed to nourish babies, and the fact that Lady Wulvedon complimented it mysteriously nourishes her self-esteem now…

The enormous mirror – its dark wooden frame nearly a foot wide and intricately carved to look like tangled vines – is tilted slightly away from the wall like a clear rectangular wave about to break over her. It reflects her entire body, along with a good portion of the room, and should it fall off the wall now it would crush her. Isabella has always had a practical mind combined with an insatiable curiosity, which leads her to conclude the nail driven into the stone must be nearly as long as a person in order to support the formidable weight of an impressive amount of sand blown into a thick reflective glass and then framed by part of a dead tree. For some reason she finds this thought oddly exciting… perhaps because one of her hands has slipped down from her breasts and is fingering the warm, slick and unfathomably deep space between her thighs. Her body has a secret mouth just like Lady Wulvedon's, except the bush protecting hers is black and not as neatly trimmed. Touching herself, she thinks about the haunting treat Bridget gave her… it was like a red flower blooming open for her tongue, which flicked swift as a humming bird's wings seeking out the delicious nectar glistening in its dark heart…

Isabella very much wants to know what Lady Wulvedon felt in those moments when she clamped her legs possessively around her head. She clearly experienced something out of the ordinary, something with all the symptoms of great pain, and yet she cried 'Oh yes' as though overcome by intense pleasure, which leads Isabella to wonder how she would feel if somebody started eating *her* like that…

Her body seems to be of the opinion it would enjoy being eaten, because the silent mouth between her thighs – which might have something quite interesting to say when given a tongue to speak with – is mysteriously salivating at the prospect of being treated like food by someone like Bridget… or her twin brother.

Suddenly thinking about him, Isabella sucks in her breath as her fingertips brush the sensitive little pearl of flesh crowning her sea-scented cleft. Lady Wulvedon's was bigger and fleshier, and she examines hers more firmly now, wondering why it feels different, even as she attempts to picture Bridget as a man with dark hair… and makes a small, helpless sound realizing she has already seen him. His must be the tall, lean figure she glimpsed yesterday shortly after she arrived. She does not know why, but she is sure it was him, and the more boldly she caresses herself the more positive she becomes the man she saw disappear into the stone wall surrounding the Castle is indeed its lord and master. She also does not understand why this certainty excites her as it does, yet she has no desire to explain away the intensely wonderful feeling the thought arouses inside her. She looks up at her slender body in the monstrous mirror, and watches her hand working between her thighs, almost with a life of its own. Vaguely, she knows she is wasting time; she should be getting dressed and preparing today's lesson, but she is in the midst of learning something herself, something that feels very important…

The budding knowledge of the divine sensations buried in her flesh flushes Isabella's cheeks and makes her eyes glow as she takes herself in – her lovely breasts crowning the hourglass of her waist and hips, her slender arms and legs, and her black hair falling tangled, vine-like over her pale skin, since she has not yet brushed it this morning. And at the same time she is seeing Lord Wulvedon's long, relaxed strides silhouetted against the western horizon. The exquisite feeling rising inside her directly between her legs intensifies as she remembers the aura of power he emanated… his silhouette the conscious embodiment of all the impenetrable shadows thrusting across the luminous grass…

'Oh my God!' she gasps as an overwhelmingly beautiful agony slices up through her body, forcing her down into the nearest chair as her knees give way beneath her.

Breathless, she raises her moist fingertips to her face and discovers her vaginal juices smell as good as Lady Wulvedon's, perhaps even better.

Isabella is finding it difficult to concentrate on the lesson for several reasons, three of which are sitting around Bridget beneath the ancient oak tree. True to her word that she would not keep Isabella confined to her windowless room, Lady Wulvedon is having her new tutor instruct her outdoors, and the beauty of the day is the biggest distraction of all. The land is enjoying a glorious spell of warmth in the normally snowbound month of December. However, a persistent chill in the sunlit air, which becomes a penetrating cold when the wind chances to blow, and the massive tree's naked limbs, make it impossible to forget it is really winter. Isabella thinks they really should not be out here, and shifts restlessly on the root she is using as a stool. Her skirt and petticoat cannot protect her soft bottom cheeks from its uneven hardness, and she does not quite know what to do with her legs. If she stretches them out in front of her, she gets tired of holding her back straight, and if she crosses them, her skirt and undergarments get all tangled up.

'Isabella, dear, the solution is to lift your dress up out of the way.' Lady Wulvedon is idly combing the long blonde hair of the girl on her right with her hands, apparently enjoying the soft, tangled curls more than trying to do anything about them.

Another young woman lying between the gnarled fingers of two massive roots with her head cradled in Lady Wulvedon's lap smiles lazily up at Isabella.

She quickly looks back down at the book she was reading from and attempts to find her place again.

'Elaine, you and Rose go help Isabella get comfortable,' Bridget commands languidly.

The girls sitting on either side of Lady Wulvedon rise gracefully. They are both tall and slender, and looking at them makes the words Isabella was attempting to focus on seem meaningless as little black bugs crawling across the page. Elaine is the one with the waving blonde hair, and her high-cut, long-sleeved dress is the same delicate blue of the sky. It fits her upper body like a glove while the long skirt flares softly down over her legs. Rose's hair is even more unruly, and a stunning auburn color matched by the dark-red of her gown, which barely covers her delicate breasts and is gathered up in a bloom of material just beneath her bosom, from which the ankle-length skirt descends in lush folds.

Both young women smile down at Isabella as she studies the soft brushstrokes of color on their lips and cheekbones. It fascinates her that these girls have treated their bodies like unfinished works of art by painting themselves, and they are both so strikingly beautiful she has no problem believing their soft mortal clay was shaped by divine intention. If it is true God created man in his own image, then woman must be what he *wished* he looked like. This is the sacrilegious thought crossing Isabella's mind as Elaine, her gray eyes narrowing mischievously, snatches the book out of her hands. Rose then grasps both her hands in hers and pulls her to her feet. Laughing happily, she reaches down and lifts Isabella's dress all the way up to her waist, exposing the knee-high white socks she is wearing inside little white lace-up boots. At the same time, Elaine puts her hands firmly on Isabella's shoulders and forces her back down.

She gasps as her soft bottom makes abrupt contact with the hard root again, and the rough bark scrapes her tender skin as she tries to close her legs and straighten out her knees, which are bent on either side of her and offering Lady Wulvedon a shamefully clear view of her pussy.

'Oh no you do not,' Elaine whispers in her ear, crouching down beside her and holding on to one of her knees as Rose similarly braces herself on the other. They force her to keep her legs open as the third girl narrows her eyes and raises her head from Bridget's lap like a cat suddenly spying a juicy mouse.

'You have a lovely little slit, Isabella,' Lady Wulvedon remarks, 'and I am tired of that dull old book you were reading from. It is truly frightening how much has been written by dried up old men, and you have spent entirely too much time in their company, I fear. Fortunately for you, I have decided that besides teaching me Latin and History, you will also serve me.'

Isabella thinks wistfully of the glorious library she has yet to see.

'Would you like that, Isabella? Would you like to be one of my girls?'

In her mind's eye she sees Lord Wulvedon striding into the Castle. 'I do not know, mistress.' She remembers the mysterious flavor of power her soul tasted watching him. 'What would I have to do?'

'What you did for me yesterday was serve me, Isabella, and although other ways will not be as pleasant, you will enjoy them just as much, or perhaps even more, simply because you will be giving me pleasure. Very soon, Isabella, although what I am about to tell you will sound exceedingly strange to you and you will certainly not believe a word of it, pleasing me will be all you care about in this world. It will come to be the only thing that matters to you at all. Obeying my commands, doing whatever I ask of you without question or reservation, never thinking of yourself but only, and always, of me, this will fill you with a happiness such as you have never known. And the harder I am on you, the more selfishly I use you, the happier you will be. Your one and only desire will be to serve me in any way I choose. Night and day you will long only to be with me. The thought of your beautiful, demanding, yet also generous and considerate mistress, will consume you. Not only your heart but your very soul will belong to me, Isabella.'

'My soul belongs to God,' she says firmly.

Rose giggles, and the nameless girl lying at Lady Wulvedon's feet suddenly begins crawling towards Isabella. She almost looks angry, and yet that is not quite the right word to describe her expression. Her lips are parted slightly and her dark eyes are half closed, as though she truly is a hungry cat smelling out its prey. The ends of her glossy brown hair trail across the earth and her sleeveless white dress is so tight, her body seems dipped in a rich cream about to drip off her nipples.

Sitting on the tree root with her skirt crumpled up around

her waist and her legs held wide open, Isabella's heart starts beating fast. At the moment, she really *does* feel like a young bird fallen out of its nest and hypnotized into breathless immobility by the dangerously beautiful creature's approach. She cannot believe – or is it that she cannot dare to hope? – she is about to be eaten alive now in the same way she devoured Lady Wulvedon yesterday. The mere possibility overwhelms her, as does how much she longs to press that lovely face against her. The desire scares her, yet even more frightening is how disappointed she will be if she cannot kiss those exquisite features with her secret nether lips. She is aware of the almost sinister crack between her thighs waiting hungrily, and getting so warm wanting to be kissed by the curving mouth approaching it that a sudden cold breeze sends a chill up her spine it feels so delicious. The wind's caress sends a ripple of pleasure through her blood and makes her shamefully aware of how wet and deep her body's mysterious rift is becoming, watching the beautiful girl crawl closer.

Crouching beside her, Elaine and Rose also appear entranced by the vision of heavy breasts swinging slowly back and forth as their owner makes her way on all fours towards them. Isabella licks her dry lips, imagining gathering the heavy globes in her hands and sucking on the yieldingly hard nipples, but it is only a fleeting desire consumed as she is by the prospect of bandaging her deliciously aching slit with those soft, curving lips…

'Do you want her, Isabella?' Lady Wulvedon asks casually.

'Yes,' she whispers, shocked by how desperate her pussy is to feel its delicious juices flowing into the other girl's mouth; by how vividly she can picture pressing the bridge of the girl's nose hard against her then grabbing the soft mane of her hair and selfishly riding her tongue into the incredibly beautiful realm of sensation she discovered this morning touching herself…

'Well, you cannot have her.' Bridget claps her hands once, and the girl who was about to give Isabella's pussy a curious lick immediately gets to her feet, scrapes dirt off her immaculate dress, and returns to sit beside her mistress. 'You have to earn your pleasures, Isabella.' Lady Wulvedon's smile is decidedly cruel.

Rose giggles again as she and Elaine also return to sit beside their mistress.

Isabella rises with as much dignity as she can muster, and smoothes her skirt down as she says coolly, 'If you are tired of the book I was using for your philosophy lesson, Bridget, we will take instruction from another.'

Rose giggles again, but then gives Lady Wulvedon an uncertain glance as Elaine winks at Isabella. The nameless girl continues to regard her with the brooding look Isabella finds so distracting as she selects the book she has in mind from a small pile she brought outside with her, and then once more seats herself on the root, this time stretching her legs out before her and holding her back straight. She clears her throat and holds the book up in front of her face to block her view of Bridget. Lady Wulvedon is looking even more strikingly beautiful this morning, in a sleeveless black gown with a full skirt that allows her to sit quite comfortably. A black scarf wrapped around her throat falls over one of her bare white shoulders, her long hair has been swept severely back away from her face and bound with a black ribbon so it flows over her other shoulder like a horse's tail, and her thin lips glisten a dark-red. Whatever she uses to color them looks disturbingly like fresh blood, an effect Isabella suspects is deliberate. She clears her throat. 'Society was originally a matriarchy,' she announces.

'A *what?*' Elaine asks.

'A matriarchy,' Bridget repeats patiently.

'What is that?' Rose sounds skeptical.

'A matriarchy is a world run by women,' Lady Wulvedon explains. 'Now be quiet so she may continue.'

'We are currently living in a patriarchal system,' Isabella informs them, 'and have been for thousands of years, although some philosophers believe this is part of a cycle and that one day we will return to a matriarchal way of life again.'

'Hmm.' Bridget sounds as though she approves of this theory.

'The fact that men and women are different is obvious,' Isabella pauses to quickly flip through the pages of a chapter in search of the passage she has in mind, 'and some philosophers believe these physical differences reflect much more profound differences that are metaphysical in nature, a reflection, as it were, of the principles of being itself, light and dark, earth and sky, fire and water, and so on and so forth. According to Weininger, '*Woman is nothing but sexuality*,' she begins reading from the book, '*whereas the true man is sexual but something else as well. There is a profound symbolic meaning in the anatomical and bodily facts that the male sexual organs seem to be something limited, detached, whereas the sexual organs of a woman go deep into her innermost flesh. As there exists in man a certain gap between himself and sexuality, he can know his own sexuality, whereas woman can be unaware of it and deny it, for she is nothing other than sexuality and is sexuality itself. A Hindu name for woman is "kamini", or "she who is made of desire", and that expresses the same meaning as the old Latin proverb,* tota mulier sexus: the

41

whole of woman is sex.' She pauses to peer over the edge of the book.

All three girls are looking at Lady Wulvedon, who is staring fixedly over at the sprawling bulk of the Castle. Isabella is beginning to wonder if she was even listening when she remarks, 'Interesting. Go on, please.'

Isabella does so eagerly. 'Weininger believes there are two types of women, those who follow Demeter and those who follow Aphrodite, or in other words, the way of the Mother and the way of the Lover.' She turns her eyes down to the book again. *'The mother type seeks man for the child, whereas the lover type seeks him for the erotic experience by itself. Thus the maternal type fits specifically into the natural order of things, whereas the pure lover type transcends this order in a certain way, and we would say that, rather than a principle that befriends and affirms the physical, earthly life, the lover type is potentially hostile to that life because of the virtual content of transcendence proper to the absolute display of Eros. Thus, although it may disappoint bourgeois morality, it is not as a mother but as a lover that woman can approach a higher order in a natural way, that is, not on the basis of ethics but merely by arousing a spontaneous disposition of her being.'\**

'Fascinating.' Lady Wulvedon rewards her with such a broad smile her fine mouth makes Isabella think of the edge of a blood-soaked blade. 'I had no idea there were such astute philosophers out there. But I think that is enough for today. It is getting rather chilly out and I do not want my girls catching cold. And you, my surprisingly clever young tutor, must still be tired after your long journey, so I will allow you to have the rest of the day off.'

'Oh mistress, thank you. May I visit the library?'

42

'No.'

The word affects Isabella like a blow. 'Why not?' she asks weakly, dazed by the finality of Bridget's tone.

'You dare to question me, Isabella?'

'No, mistress, I just wondered why I cannot—'

'Isabella!' Lady Wulvedon holds her arms out before her and Elaine and Rose immediately scramble to their feet to help her up.

Clutching the book to her chest with one hand, Isabella quickly pushes herself to her feet with the other.

Bridget walks over to her, grips her chin between her thumb and forefinger, and looks her straight in the eye. 'If you ever question me again, Isabella, I will have to punish you severely.'

The fear of losing her new position and having no references and no money and nowhere else to go is a lump in her throat that will not let her speak, even as her soul screams out in protest at the thought of being denied access to what she is sure is a magnificent library.

'Do you understand, Isabella?'

She wants to scream 'No!' instead of whispering, 'Yes, my lady.' Yet her soul is burning like the sun rising behind the dark mountain of Lady Wulvedon's power over her, and she cannot stop herself from adding, 'I understand, but I will ask you again tomorrow.'

# Chapter Three

Isabella discovers having the rest of the day off constitutes a form of punishment; since there is nothing she can do with her time except remain inside her luxurious bedroom.

She seeks to entertain herself by moving from table to table, examining all the curious and exquisite little objects cluttering them. The Wulvedon family must have traveled far and wide through the centuries because, as far as she can tell, none of the artifacts seem to come from the same time or place.

Still frowning her frustration at not being in the library right now – which she pictures as oval in shape with several tiers of books accessible only by long and dangerous ladders – she picks up a little laughing Buddha carved from a slick, light-green stone. She has seen paintings and drawings of such curious idols, but never actually held one in her hand and felt its reality. It makes her incredulous to think people actually worship such silly things. The little fat man sitting cross-legged on her palm is completely unaffected by her mental scorn, however, and she knows, of course, it is the qualities he embodies the people who fashion such an object revere, not the statue itself. Still, it annoys her that he seems to find her situation so amusing.

Sighing, she sets him back down gently and turns to face the door again. It is not locked. She could disobey Lady Wulvedon and leave her room and go in search of the library, but chances are she would never find it and she would lose her position, which she has to keep reminding herself she cannot afford to do, as well as be punished for her transgression.

She crosses her arms in growing frustration, and leans back against the table. She does not really want to, but she cannot help wondering what Bridget meant when she said she would punish her severely if she questioned her again. Would she leave her locked up in here with only enough bread and water to survive? Certainly there are laws against treating a governess in such a way. Yet who would even know? The Castle is a veritable stone fortress and she has no living relatives to ask after her health; anything could happen to her here and no one would ever know or care.

She steals a furtive glance to her right and sees her own worried face gazing back at her. Her hair is neatly contained in a braid hanging down her back like a thick rope. Seeing it, she tells herself it would behoove her to take her emotions similarly in hand. She should be grateful she found this position, which pays much better than most and provides her with such beautiful surroundings instead of a plain little room. She needs to remember her situation. Bridget is right, it is not her place to question the lady of the house when she is little more than a servant herself.

Her frown deepening, Isabella's arms fall to her sides as she walks slowly towards the door.

Why is she not allowed to leave her room? She is a teacher, not a servant, and certainly she is not a prisoner. What on earth could Lady Wulvedon have meant when she said she would not be responsible for what happened to her if she wandered out of her room unattended? What could possibly happen to her inside the Castle? Even if she does by some miracle come upon the library, she can simply resist the urge to enter it and, therefore, not actually disobey her beautiful student's cruel and irrational wish to deny her access to the treasure of all those books.

As she pulls open the heavy door, Isabella tells herself she should not be doing this, but a willful and intensely curious part of her does not listen.

It is slightly warmer out in the corridor. Her high-ceilinged room is cold as a cavern reached by way of a maze of shadowy stone passages. It is beyond her comprehension how Lady Wulvedon found her way back into this windowless wing of the Castle from the wonderfully bright and airy chambers opening out onto the world. The tutor's room may be sumptuous, but it is still decidedly in the servant's quarters, as no one would ever willingly deny themselves the joy of sunrise and birdsong, or the melancholy beauty of sunset and moonlight's caress across their bed.

The door closes from its own weight behind her, with a click like a disapproving tongue and a thud that reverberates in her chest as she suddenly finds it difficult to catch her breath. She should not be doing this. She is disobeying Lady Wulvedon's direct order…

Isabella lifts her white skirt and turns left simply because it is the opposite direction Bridget took this morning when she came for her. Every few yards, a torch is thrust into a metal holder set in the stone wall, leaving long stretches of flickering shadows deepening almost into absolute darkness at the farthest point between each small blaze. The fire-blackened walls and ceiling make her question this dramatically inefficient form of lighting. Surely gas lamps would make more sense, but then who is she to question such eccentric housekeeping?

The quiet ticking of her square heels on the stone floor is barely audible over the crackling sound of live and hungry flames devouring the wooden shafts sustaining them. She is so nervous, Isabella finds herself comparing her soul to these torches, for it, too, is gradually burning out her body. And what will become of her soul then? She often wonders if all her thoughts and feelings are destined to an eternal darkness in which she will not even remember she ever existed, and the inconceivable possibility inevitably makes her shudder. She has no idea where she is going, already it seems as though she has been walking for a long time, and it frightens her how alone she seems to be in this fiery maze of narrow and seemingly endless passages. Yet she refuses to turn back. She cannot turn back, not until she has gone just a little farther. She is about to turn a corner when she hears a soft moan, and stops dead, her hands clenched into fists around her skirt as she holds herself perfectly still, listening. The last torch she passed is far behind her and she is cloaked in darkness. The shadows dancing on the wall of the corridor intersecting with hers tell her there is another torch nearby, but the breathless sounds she is hearing are coming from a human throat.

Her heart beating violently, Isabella peers cautiously around the corner.

A man is standing a few feet away and a girl is kneeling before him.

She quickly presses herself back against the cold stone, not quite understanding, or believing, what she just saw. Her bosom heaves as she tries to control her breathing, which sounds incredibly loud to her. Yet a small part of her mind calmly assures her they will not hear her over the crackling of the fire they are standing beneath, and that they will not notice if she looks again…

The man's hands are resting on the girl's head, his black-gloved fingers distinctly visible against her golden hair. Isabella can only see his profile, but her pulse seems to trip over itself as she recognizes him. There is no question his is the same tall, lean figure she saw walking so confidently against the burning sunset. Now he is standing motionless inside a torch's glowing sphere, but he is not completely still, for his hips are swaying gently back and forth…

Isabella plants her back against the wall again and closes her eyes for a moment to try and rein in her racing pulse, but then she cannot resist – she *has* to take another look.

The girl is bracing herself on the man's thighs, which blend with the darkness in black leather leggings. Her eyes are squeezed shut and she moans as over and over again he slips a strangely glistening rod slowly in and out of her mouth. Isabella cannot believe it, but she suddenly realizes what she is seeing caressed by firelight and shadow is an erect penis. She has studied illustrations of the male sexual organ in biology texts, but it was always sketched in black-and-white and she had believed it to be much smaller. Its actual size, vivid pink color and shimmering rigidity, enthralls her as much as it shocks her. Ancient statues deceived her by depicting a limp organ scarcely bigger than an acorn resting harmlessly against small testicles. Lord Wulvedon's balls are hidden inside his black leather leggings, but there is more than enough for her to look at as he patiently yet relentlessly penetrates the lovely tortured face on a level with his hips. Then the girl suddenly opens her eyes to gaze up at him, and Isabella understands that even though she must be making a terrible effort not to gag, it is not agony she is experiencing at all, but something much more intense. Profoundly confused by the girl's expression, Isabella stops trying to think at all and simply watches Lord Wulvedon – because surely it is him – feeding his impressive erection in and out of the kneeling girl's devoted mouth… and finds her pulse mysteriously falling into rhythm with him…

Her heart beating to the sight of his hips swaying back and forth hypnotizes her into almost forgetting where she is, and that she should not be there, his long, glistening shaft blinding her to everything else as over and over again she watches it totally consumed by the warm and wet hole of the girl's mouth. Then abruptly he grabs her even more firmly by the hair and moves her face swiftly up and down the full length of his rigid cock. Then he thrusts his hips remorselessly into her face and throws his head back.

Isabella does not so much hear as feel his groan deep inside her, and seeing his knees buckle slightly her own nearly give way. Her pussy is painfully hot and wet, darkening her mind with a longing she has no words for, and the flames above his head seem to burn directly between her legs for a blinding moment.

She remains breathlessly rooted to the spot, unable to take her eyes off his magnificent manhood as he pulls it out of the girl's mouth. She does not seem to want to let him go, however, because she licks him passionately and moans even more desperately.

He steps back out of her reach. 'I told you not to follow me,' he reprimands her, and his deep, stern voice captures all of Isabella's attention.

The girl literally throws herself at his feet and wraps her bare arms around his black boots, her hair a golden carpet he could easily walk over if he wanted to. 'Please forgive me, my lord, *please*,' she begs.

He manages to sheathe his still rather stiff penis back inside his leggings. 'No.' He imbues the word with even more heart-stopping finality than his sister.

'Oh my lord, please,' she sobs, '*please* forgive me.' She looks beseechingly up at his hard face. 'Please,' she whispers, 'please do not send me away. Give me another chance, my lord.'

Isabella holds her breath, waiting for his response.

'I told you not to follow me, Juliet.'

'Oh God, I know, but it has been so long since I saw you, my lord… I just *had* to be with you. I could not bear it when all you said was "good afternoon, Juliet" and then just walked away. I mean, how could you do that? It was so… so cruel!'

'Why do you want to stay with me, Juliet, if I am so cruel?'

This strikes Isabella as a reasonable question.

'Because I love you, my lord.' Tears stream down her pretty face. 'I love you! Please punish me, but do not send me away, please, I could not bear it.' She rests her forehead on his boots and closes her eyes. 'I could not bear it…' She appears utterly worn out by the intensity of her emotions.

'Get up,' he says shortly.

She obeys him at once, and then stands before him with her head bowed and her hands clasped behind her back.

'What good would it do to punish you if you have *asked* me to punish you, Juliet?' He tilts her head up with his index finger and makes her look at him. 'What purpose would it serve if it is what you wish?'

'But I do not wish to be punished, my lord, I—'

'Excuse me, but did you not ask me to punish you?'

'Yes, my lord, because anything is better than you sending me away.' She sounds confused and yet also more hopeful.

He turns her head from side to side like an artist studying his model before he goes to work, but Isabella knows he is examining the girl's face after dipping into the mysterious medium of her feelings and stroking them with his male tool. 'That means the only way to truly punish you is to send you away, Juliet,' he concludes.

'I will die if you send me away, my lord,' she says with quiet fervor. 'I will die.'

'No, you will not.' He lets go of her. 'However, you can stay, for now.'

'Oh my lord, thank you,' she ardently addresses his boots. 'Thank you!'

'But you will be punished for this, Juliet, make no mistake about that. You have made me late for an important appointment.'

'I am sorry, my lord.'

'Oh, you will be sorry, my girl,' he turns away, 'very sorry, indeed.'

Isabella presses herself back against the wall and holds her breath as he passes just inches away from her on his way down the left wing of the corridor. Once he is out of sight, she does not wait to see where the girl goes but immediately begins running as quietly as she can all the way back to her room.


'What is the matter with you today, Isabella? That is the third time you have lost your place on the page.' Lady Wulvedon's tone is an unsettling blend of sympathy and impatience, in the same way her relaxed smile does not quite match the cat-like alertness of her body. She is wearing yet another sleeveless bodice. This one is yellow and embroidered with stylized white vines that appear to bloom in her breasts, which are distractingly full and heavy considering her slender frame. Her long skirt is a glossy black and rustles sensually as she shifts restlessly in the same chair where she sat to give Isabella her special treat.

'I am sorry, mistress,' she gives up trying to focus on the small black print in favor of meeting her student's slightly slanted eyes, 'but I am finding it difficult to concentrate.'

Bridget toys idly with a lock of hair curled like an inverted question mark over her cleavage. 'And why is that, my dear?'

For perhaps the hundredth time, Isabella suffers a hot flash like a knife thrust swiftly in and out of her belly as she recalls the scene in the torch-lit corridor. She cannot seem to think about anything else, and what it makes her feel leaves her feeling weak and breathless, as if her soul is slipping mysteriously away from her and there is nothing she can do about it. Obviously she cannot tell Lady Wulvedon the truth – that she watched her brother shoving his cock into a girl's mouth yesterday when she left her room without permission. 'Because, my lady, I keep wondering what you meant when you said you would have to punish me severely if I ever questioned you again.' She is in fact wondering how Lord Wulvedon plans to punish that girl. 'May I see the library?' she asks bluntly.

Bridget rolls her eyes up towards the ceiling and her smile deepens as though she suddenly glimpses an adorable flock of cherubs fluttering in the shadows. 'No,' she says indulgently, as if the invisible winged infants are threatening some divine mischief.

Isabella bites her lip and manages to stop herself from demanding why not, and instead she says, 'Very well, mistress, I will ask you again tomorrow.'

'If you ask me again tomorrow, I will have to punish you for annoying me, Isabella.'

'Are you and your brother in the habit of punishing people for no good reason?' she retorts, thinking no appointment could possibly be more important than how much that poor girl obviously loves him.

Her back straightening, Bridget's smile vanishes

completely. 'What has my brother got to do with this?'

'Nothing.' She quickly looks back down at the page she was reading from. 'I was simply wondering if the reason you will not let me see the library is because your brother told you not to let me.'

'Excuse me?' Lady Wulvedon rises angrily. '*No* one tells me what to do. Do I make myself absolutely clear?'

'Yes, mistress,' she answers meekly, but then asks without thinking, 'Is that why you never wish to marry?'

Bridget grasps her skirt with both hands as if preparing to storm out of the room in the face of such effrontery from a mere servant. Then her expression and posture soften as she stares into Isabella's wide, honey-brown eyes, and her smile returns as if she finds the infinite curiosity she sees in them so sweet it cancels out the bitter taste left in her mouth by the mere idea of someone trying to tell her what to do. 'Yes,' she admits, and sits down again, reclining informally in the throne-like chair, 'that is precisely why I never intend to marry.'

It does not escape Isabella's notice that she replaces 'wish' with 'intend'. 'But what if you fall in love?' She could not fall asleep last night as she kept hearing that poor girl sobbing, 'Because I love you, my lord, I love you'.

'Isabella,' Bridget's good humor has apparently returned, 'love is like a hole in the ground. If you are not spinning dreams in the clouds, but always look where you are going, you will not fall into it like so many silly fools do. You will, if you are wise, walk around it, and past it. What people do not realize is that they make the decision to fall in love.' She raises her right hand before her to admire the large heavy rings adorning all her fingers. 'They choose to let their emotional and mental defenses down so love seems to descend upon them like a sickness they can do nothing about.'

Isabella has never thought of love as a physical illness, yet it makes sense considering the painfully intense stab of feeling she experiences whenever she remembers the way Lord Wulvedon's gloved hands held that girl's head. 'But that is just an image,' she argues, 'love is not actually a hole in the earth.' Her own eyes shine as in her mind's eye she sees tears streaming down Juliet's lovely face. 'It seems more like a hole in the soul,' she muses out loud.

Lady Wulvedon turns a ring with a large red stone around and around on her finger as she studies her young teacher's face. 'Well,' she says finally, 'if your soul belongs to God, as you believe it does, then should not *His* love be enough to fill it?'

'Yes, it should be…'

'But it is not?' She smiles smugly down at her ring.

'I did not say—'

'Your eyes speak more eloquently than words.' She raises her arms over her head and idly grasps the carved back of the chair, which causes her dress to slip down so low Isabella holds her breath hoping to see her nipples rise over the bodice's curving hills like two rosy suns, for she truly enjoyed looking at Lady Wulvedon's naked breasts. 'And right now your eyes are telling me,' Bridget continues contentedly, 'that you have something on your mind today, something that is greatly preoccupying your thoughts. Would you be so kind,' she shifts her hips, getting even more comfortable, 'telling me what it is?'

'I told you, mistress, I was wondering what you meant by *severe punishment*.'

'Mm, yes, but that is not all you are thinking about.'

'No, that is not all I am thinking about,' she admits, gazing with growing hunger at the white globes of Lady Wulvedon's breasts inexorably rising like dough, which at any moment will swell right out of the bodice's stiff crust…

'Of course it is not, Isabella.' She sounds pleased. 'You are thinking, perhaps, about the special treat I gave you the evening you arrived?'

'Yes,' she whispers, profoundly relieved her secret is safe for now.

'Well, it pleases me you are thinking about it, Isabella.'

'It pleases me that I am pleasing you, mistress.' She looks back down at the little black words marching across the page. 'But I do not understand.'

'Of course you do not. There is so much you do not understand yet, but do not let that upset you, my dear. I told you, we are going to teach each other.'

'Thank you, my lady, but I still cannot help wondering why,' she keeps her eyes lowered humbly, 'you refuse to let me see the library.'

'Oh, Isabella.' She sighs. 'The first thing you learned was never to assume anything. The second thing you must learn is that *why* does not matter. All that matters is what *I* desire. If I desire you to stand on your head you will do it, and not ask why I wish you to do it. You will do it without question simply because I told you to, and when you are further along in your training, you will enjoy doing it simply *because* I have told you to do it. There is no *why*, Isabella, there is only desire. Why are we born?' She lowers her arms. 'Why do we die?' She shrugs.

*And why*, Isabella wonders, *does Juliet want to stay with Lord Wulvedon when he is so cruel to her?*

'But what we do know for a fact is that we feel,' Bridget concludes. 'Do we not?'

'Oh yes, mistress.' Since she arrived at the Castle, she has felt things she never even dreamed she could feel.

Bridget laughs. 'You are so cute, Isabella, you have such

a lively mind. I love all my girls, but they are not very bright. They are perfectly content to sleep all day.'

'Then what do they do all night?'

Lady Wulvedon laughs as though she has never heard anything so amusing in her life. 'I think it is safe to assume,' she rests a hand over her cleavage as she catches her breath, 'you are a virgin!'

'Of course I am.' She cannot stop seeing Lord Wulvedon's glistening penis sliding in and out of the girl's mouth. 'How could you even suggest—?'

'Oh relax.' Bridget shoos her indignation away like a pesky insect. 'I was not trying to insult you, Isabella, and perhaps, if you are a very good girl and teach me many interesting things, as well as learn your own lessons well, I will let you dine with me one night soon.'

'I would be honored, mistress. Do you dine with… do you dine alone?'

'I never dine alone, Isabella. I believe I have not dined alone a single night in my entire life. Even when I was nursing at my mother's breast I was not dining alone. Oh, but I should not have said that. My poor dear,' she rises again, 'do not look so sad. That was very inconsiderate of me, I was not thinking. Here,' she reaches down into her bodice and lifts both her breasts out of the heart-shaped golden cups, 'accept them as an apology for my insensitive remark.'

Isabella scarcely notices the heavy book slipping off her lap to the floor as she gets up to cup Lady Wulvedon's breasts in her hands. She loves the heavy fullness of them, and for a lovely moment she extinguishes her memory of that torch-lit corridor as she buries her face in the deliciously deep cleavage. All her thoughts go out like so many urgent fires in the cool snowy mounds as she closes her eyes and breathes in the clean, fresh scent of Bridget's skin.

'Mm, you are a passionate little thing.' Lady Wulvedon rests her hands gently on her head. 'Do you wish to serve me, Isabella?'

She imagines Lord Wulvedon's black-gloved fingers resting on her head like this, and then gripping her skull as he pumps his rigid male organ in and out of her mouth... she gasps and takes a few stumbling steps back in a futile effort to escape the sword-thrust of feeling between her thighs, but instead of killing her the sensation makes her feel frighteningly alive. 'No,' she whispers, at last fully facing the memory of a girl kneeling and moaning before a man in a dark passage, and suddenly she is sure of something beyond a shadow of a doubt without understanding it at all. The realization is so blindingly intense it is like being struck by lightning, and as if it is going to kill her and she has nothing to lose, she looks Bridget straight in the eye and declares, 'I wish to serve your brother.'

# Chapter Four

The casually sinister phrase 'when you are further along in your training' keeps ringing in Isabella's head. What sort of training? She ponders the question, which she cannot even begin to answer, in an effort not to think about what is going to happen to her soon. She still cannot quite grasp the fact that she is on her way to Lady Wulvedon's quarters to be punished, severely.

Ludly came for her, his face a stoic mask of long-suffering indifference. 'Are you ready, miss?' he enquired with a resigned air.

'No, Ludly, I am not ready,' she replied, but even though she was standing right in front of him she could not get him to meet her eyes. She knew it was probably futile, but she could not stop herself from tugging on one of his gray sleeves and asking in a desperate whisper, 'What is Lady Wulvedon planning to do to me, Ludly? I have never been punished before. What does she mean by *severe* punishment? Has she ever punished you? Have you ever seen her punish one of her girls? Are all noble families in the habit of reprimanding their servants like this?'

His succinct reply to all her questions had been, 'Lady Wulvedon is waiting, miss, and it is not a good idea to keep her waiting.'

It was not much comfort at all, but his utterly calm demeanor, and the fact that he was apparently attempting to spare her even more severe punishment, applied a slight soothing balm to her nerves, enabling her to compose herself enough to lift her trailing hem off the floor and say, 'Very well, Ludly, lead the way.'

When he turned left outside the door her knuckles went white on her black skirt, but when they reached the spot in the corridor where Lord Wulvedon had stood and the girl had knelt, there was nothing there except her vivid memory of the sinful scene, still mysteriously smoldering in her blood just as the torch continued to burn.

Following behind Ludly now, perversely wishing he would walk faster so she can get this – whatever *this* is – over with, she tries again to understand what came over her in the moment when she told Lady Wulvedon she wished to serve her brother. She has no idea what on earth possessed her to say such a thing. She does remember, however, that she meant it with all her heart and soul, until Bridget slapped her and snapped her out of the inexplicable feeling.

Tangled up in thoughts and emotions she cannot seem to make sense of, her nerves sharp as claws sinking into her belly so she almost feels sick to her stomach with anxiety, Isabella forgets to notice which way Ludly turns whenever they come to a fork in the corridor. It seems as though they have been walking for hours when he finally pushes open a heavy black door covered with sharp silver studs.

They step out into a large open space. She takes a deep breath and looks around her, grateful to be out of the dark, low-ceilinged passages. They are in an immense covered courtyard, her boot heels clicking against a beautifully polished expanse of black and white marble tiles broken up only by a white-stone fountain. Water tinkles musically down from one circular basin into another, each one slightly larger than the last, but she is already looking up at three different levels of open hallways and the dozens of doors opening from them into countless rooms and stairwells. She has never before been inside such monumental and inspiring architecture; the church where she and her father attended services could fit here with room to spare. This is exactly how she pictured the library, only on a smaller scale and as oval in shape instead of perfectly round, with rows upon rows of books stacked all the way up to the cathedral-style ceiling. Yet when she looks up at the second level it is not old leather-bound volumes she sees, but a group of men dressed entirely in black leather talking amongst themselves.

Isabella stops walking and stares up at them, her knuckles again white as snow against her black skirt. There are four men standing at the railing, and Bridget's tall, dark-haired brother is one of them.

'Miss?' Ludly looks slowly over his shoulder at her, apparently not an easy task for his old bones. 'Lady Wulvedon is waiting,' he reminds her ominously.

'Let her wait,' she replies, and then a very strange thing happens. She literally feels her soul rise out of her body in her voice, soaring like a bird up to the balcony on the invisible wings of her swiftly beating heart as she cries, 'Lord Wulvedon!'

All the men turn their heads and look down at her.

The combined force of their direct stares makes it hard for her to breathe, much less move. Suddenly she feels like a black queen on a chessboard, as well as like a helpless pawn, in a game she cannot even begin to comprehend, and she knows – once more beyond a shadow of a doubt without being able to mentally grasp the reason for her intense certainty – that she has to make a move now because her life depends on it. 'My lord, I am your sister's new teacher.' Her voice, trained by singing hymns in church, carries nicely. 'It is time we were introduced.'

His men move aside as Lord Wulvedon steps closer to

the railing and leans over it. 'Good evening.' He smiles.

'Good evening,' she echoes.

'Come closer, *teacher*.'

She obeys him without realizing it she is so intent on trying to make out his face, which she has only seen in profile twice before. Then she makes the mistake of remembering how he flung his head back when he buried his penis deep in the girl's mouth, and is forced to stop walking as her knees go dangerously weak beneath her skirt.

'So, you are the girl who answered the advertisement.' He is still looking down at her, and yet he seems to be talking more to himself, so she does not respond. 'What is your name?' he asks, glancing at the men behind him, who all promptly join him in leaning comfortably against the railing and smiling down at her.

'Isabella,' she answers proudly, her chin already held high to look up at him.

'*Isabella...*' he savors her name. 'Gentlemen,' he glances at his men again, 'say good evening to Isabella.'

'Good evening, Isabella,' they all say in unison, and she is grateful for the excuse to curtsy as it permits her knees to buckle without appearing to do so.

'My lord,' Ludly speaks up abruptly, 'Lady Wulvedon is... *ahem*,' he clears his throat significantly. 'She is waiting, my lord.'

His smiling gaze giving way to a sober expression, Lord Wulvedon straightens up slowly.

Insanely wishing Ludly had tripped into the fountain and drowned before he spoke, Isabella takes a few more steps forward and makes another desperate move. 'Lady Wulvedon is waiting to punish me, my lord, simply because I keep asking to be allowed to visit the library,' she informs him. 'For some reason she will not explain, she refuses to even let me see it. Yet as her teacher, I feel I have a right to see it, I *must* see it, my lord, so I told her I would ask her every day until she said yes, and now she intends to punish me for annoying her.'

'My sister does as she pleases, Isabella, and a little discipline will only improve your character.'

The black and white floor seems to spin around her as disappointment leaves her thoughts and feelings reeling. The white queen has swept her off the board and she is utterly powerless. She has only one possible move left, and the fact that he is still there looking down at her fills her with a breathtaking sense of hope. In fact, his intense regard strikes her as such a blessing, her soul seems to rise out of her again as she dares to confess, 'If I am to be punished, my lord, I would rather it was by your hand.'

'I do not interfere with my sister's pleasures, Isabella.'

'But she is so angry with me because when… when she asked me if I wished to serve her I said… I said I wished to serve her brother.'

His stare, and the thoughts behind it, grip her as effectively as his fingers did that girl's head, and she gets some idea how Juliet felt as his silent regard becomes the only thing she is aware of; as it consumes her mind wondering what his response will be and fills her heart with a breathless hope such as she has never known before. Finally, his deep voice seems to flow through her blood like warm wine drunk at Christmas on an empty stomach, when he says quietly, 'I see.' He does not promise her anything at all, and yet in the haunting way which defies explanation she is sure he *has* promised her something, and her inexplicable faith in his understanding only deepens as he turns away abruptly.

His men follow him more slowly, their penetrating stares still holding hers as their soft smiles caress her in such a way that it is both a relief and a disappointment to see them go.

'What took you so long?' Lady Wulvedon demands of Ludly.

'I dragged my feet the whole way,' Isabella answers for him, 'as I have no desire to be punished, severely or otherwise.'

The old man stares into space, where he apparently sees no reason to contradict her.

'You are dismissed, Ludly.' Bridget waves him away, a gesture she appears to be fond of, and which prompts Isabella to wonder what it would be like to be able to shoo away everything disagreeable to her. Unfortunately, she could not waive the *Grim Reaper* away like a fly. How much she misses her father is bad enough, but that he also left her alone and penniless is adding all sorts of disagreeable dimensions to her unhappiness.

Ludly shuffles obediently back out through the archway opening onto this particular section of Lady Wulvedon's quarters, occupying an entire wing of the Castle, and Isabella takes a quick look around her.

Gorgeous tapestries cover every inch of the stone walls, each one worthy of hours, even days, of contemplation. She glimpses a horse and rider in full black armor, an ivy-covered tower being struck by lightning behind him, and deep forests filled with mythological beasts and tumultuous oceans – darkly magical worlds woven to keep out the damp and the cold. Three divans upholstered in gem-like colors – amethyst, ruby and sapphire – are arranged in a semicircle near one enchanted wall facing the center of the room, where a narrow black column joins the floor's dark-green tiles with the ceiling, arching high overhead and painted a dark-blue decorated with hundreds of golden stars. Chains and ropes dangle from the column, which is really nothing more than a pole, and her heart starts beating anxiously looking at it, for she has never seen anything more sinister in her life. It is the one starkly real object in the dream-like room, and now she is aware of it she cannot seem to take her eyes off it. Her body does not need to be told this unnatural metal trunk, with one end rooted in the earth-green tiles and the other vanishing into a symbolic heaven, is going to play a part in her body's punishment.

'Well, Isabella,' Lady Wulvedon smiles as though she merely invited her for tea, 'have you prepared yourself?'

'I did not know what to prepare myself for,' she replies faintly. How beautiful Bridget looks makes it difficult to be angry with her. She is wearing another black gown today, but this one clings to her body like a shadow while barely containing her breasts, and the sleeves are not attached to the dress at all, but are more like long gloves cut off at the wrists. Once again her hair is pulled severely back away from her face and hangs over one of her delicate shoulders like a horse's mane.

'Do you mean to tell me,' she walks slowly around Isabella as she speaks, looking her up and down with a slight frown, 'your father never took you over his knee and spanked you when you were a bad girl?'

'Never,' she replies indignantly. 'He was the kindest and gentlest of men.'

'There is no such thing, Isabella. Oh, he may have seemed that way to you, but the truth is all men care only for themselves, and whether they subdue you with an iron fist or a velvet glove depends both on their own temperaments and on what they know will work to control you. It is the kind and gentle ones who will usually have the most power over you, because you will not see what they are doing as clearly as when they physically abuse and beat you so you remain in your proper place.'

Isabella listens open-mouthed as Bridget's venomous vision insinuates itself around her innocent soul like a black serpent, as she continues circling her body. Already she can feel Lady Wulvedon's cynicism beginning to squeeze the hope out of her heart; the exquisite feeling she experienced staring up into Lord Wulvedon's intense eyes. She keeps remembering the way his irises caught the light streaming in through the circular glass at the ceiling's apex, which suggests they are not black but perhaps a very dark, slate-gray...

'Isabella!'

'Yes?' she gasps.

Bridget stares into her eyes for a long moment, and then abruptly claps her hands three times.

The three girls Isabella met under the old oak tree seem to glide into the room through another archway, as lovely as the three Graces in flowing Grecian style garments whose colors match the jewel-toned divans. They appear to have recently finished bathing. Their hair is still a little damp, and the fine material of their dresses clings to their nipples, bellies and thighs in slightly darker patches. They look like nymphs stepped out of one of the tapestry's woven forests, an impression intensified in Isabella's mind by the way they smile at her, their eyes glittering with an excitement that makes her nervously aware of her own very vulnerable body.

'Remove her dress,' Lady Wulvedon commands, 'and do not bother with the buttons, just rip it off her.'

Isabella cannot believe she heard Bridget correctly, which is why she resists the urge to run. She would not have gotten very far anyway, for the girls fall upon her at once. She thinks wildly of Dionysus and his Maenads and then of a small black beetle she once saw drowning in a puddle reflecting a rainbow as they grab her by the collar and sleeves, and begin wrenching her back and forth between them. Her dress was made for cold winters days and is not easy to rip, but finally they manage to tear it open down the front and instantly proceed to peel her out of it with a fierce efficiency that dazes her.

'Stop!' she cries as they make short work of her white slip, their laughter ripping what remains of her dignity away with it.

'Oh stop sniveling, Isabella.' Bridget sounds exasperated. 'I told you I was going to have that hideous thing burned.'

She closes her eyes and wraps her arms around herself, trembling not from cold but because she suddenly does not know who she is anymore. She bought this dress the day after her father died, and now it is as though everything she has thought and felt since then, all her love and her grief, have been stripped from her. She cannot bear to look at the black shreds of cloth littering the floor. They strike her as her own fragmented shadow as fear, despair, anger and outrage block the sun of what was always her positive outlook on life and her faith in other peoples' good intentions.

'Let us not waste any more time,' Lady Wulvedon says shortly. 'Take her to the tree.'

*The tree?* Isabella thinks numbly, opening her eyes again, but she does not resist as three claw-like hands grab her arms and pull her towards the black pole. Strangely enough, she is almost relieved. She is going to find out now what members of the nobility consider severe punishment. She will not have to wonder and worry about it anymore. The sun will set and then rise again tomorrow like every other day and nothing will be different except for the fact that she will know what it feels like to be severely punished. She stokes her courage with this reasoning, and it works until her arms are yanked straight up over her head and a rope is wrapped so tightly around her wrists she winces in pain. 'Oh God, that hurts!' she exclaims. 'Not so tight, please.'

'Be quiet,' Elaine hisses in her ear.

'Who do you think you are, anyway?' Rose adds disdainfully. 'Do you think you are special just because you know a few big words?'

Their hostility leaves her speechless. She cannot understand what she has done to deserve it, and her head starts spinning again trying to think of what she might have said. But then the pole pressing against her body demands all her attention it is so cold and hard. The unyielding metal puts an uncomfortable pressure on the bone between her breasts and digs into her belly as the nameless girl slips a heavy chain around her waist, securing her firmly against it.

Lady Wulvedon steps into her line of sight. 'You are an extremely willful and stubborn young woman, Isabella, and worst of all you believe what you want matters. I am teaching you an important life lesson here today. Today you will learn what you want matters not at all. One way or the other, the world will have its way with you, Isabella, but I can help protect you. I can give you a beautiful home, beautiful friends, beautiful clothes, beautiful dishes to satisfy your hunger every night, and beautiful vintages and beautiful sensations to fulfill an even deeper hunger. All I ask in return is that you obey me without question. You do not wish me to send you away without any references, in disgrace. You do not want that, do you, Isabella?'

'No!' she sobs, ashamed but unable to prevent the tears streaming down her face and dripping onto her breasts in hot punctuation of Lady Wulvedon's cold statements.

'Of course it is not what you want.' Bridget smiles and reaches up to finish unraveling Isabella's braid, allowing her thick hair to flow freely down her back. 'Therefore, I will ask you again. This is the third and final time I will ask you. Do you wish to serve me, Isabella?'

Even with her eyes filled with tears and Bridget's radiant beauty, she sees Lord Wulvedon leaning against the railing and smiling down at her... Lord Wulvedon staring intently down into her eyes before he turned away abruptly... Lord Wulvedon... Lord Wulvedon... 'Yes,' she whispers, closing her eyes as she realizes she has just chosen to remain in the Castle of her own free will. She was told she could pack her bags and leave or do a mysterious thing called *serve*, and she chose what seemed like the lesser of two evils. Because she has no idea what she is getting herself into here, whereas she knows very well what awaits her out in the world, penniless and alone. And because if she did not say 'yes' to Lady Wulvedon now, she would never see her brother again...

'Say it, Isabella,' all the patience is gone from Bridget's voice, 'and look me in the eye as you do so.'

Her fingertips tingle as her hands begin going numb, and Lady Wulvedon's will is having a similar effect on her feelings, which are as trapped as her body. 'I wish to serve you,' she declares miserably.

Bridget rests her right hand gently on her wet cheek and looks earnestly into her eyes. 'I will care for you, Isabella. I will cherish you for who you are. My brother would only use your body, and then throw you away. He is like a wolf, Isabella. He thrives on fresh meat. He lives for the hunt and the thrill of the kill. He would leave only your bones in his wake.'

'My God,' she gasps, 'how can you say such things

about your own brother?'

Lady Wulvedon's lips fall over hers. They are firm yet soft, and because she has never been kissed on the mouth before, Isabella's breath catches in surprise at the yielding yet demanding sensation. When Bridget's tongue thrusts into her mouth she tries to pull back, but she cannot, and she moans to feel herself pinned to the spot unable to resist this tender but insistent invasion. The experience is not hurting her, however, and there is actually something oddly pleasurable about it. Being kissed like this feels like an intensely intimate conversation; she is fast learning the tongue is perfectly capable of expressing thoughts and feelings without the need for words. Her mistress is angry, she senses this in the way Bridget's tongue circles hers relentlessly, as if determined to take her breath away and overwhelm her. And she succeeds for a moment, until Isabella begins pouring her own passionately determined soul into the kiss.

Lady Wulvedon lets go of her face and steps back. 'Oh Isabella,' she breathes. Then her eyes harden and she moves away. 'Use the cane,' she says shortly.

'But she has never been beaten before, mistress,' Elaine protests.

'Precisely. This one needs to be completely broken before I can begin her training, so break her, no mercy.' Bridget walks over to the central ruby-red divan and reclines across it, her figure a curving black horizon as Elaine and Rose make themselves comfortable on the lounges to either side of her.

The pain seems to come from nowhere and everywhere at once, and Isabella screams because she simply cannot believe it. Then it hits her again and she is thoroughly convinced it is real, more real than anything she has ever felt before. She completely forgets the minor torments of her tingling hands and aching wrists, which are as nothing compared to the anguish inflicted by the cane. The knife-sharp stick slicing into the tender cheeks of her bottom makes it impossible for her to think. All she can do is feel, and all she feels is agony. She is only vaguely aware of crying, 'Stop! Oh God, stop, please, stop!' as screaming and breathing become one terrible and inescapable necessity. Yet the three lovely figures reclining a dream-like distance away remain as unmoved by her distress as statues. She thinks if effigies on an ancient Etruscan sarcophagus, because she cannot possibly survive one more lick of that evil stick. Then the cruel goddess in black lifts a hand to point down, and Isabella discovers she still did not really know what pain was at all. When the cane strikes the back of her thighs her knees give way, surrendering on behalf of her entire body. But the rope around her wrists and the chain around her waist hold her up, forcing her to endure yet more blinding strokes of the evil stick, and everything else ceases to exist as the torment seems to permeate not only to her bones but her very soul. The agony is so impossibly deep and intense the whole room begins spiraling into it…

'Stop, she has had enough.'

'Should we take her down?'

'No, leave her hanging there for a bit, she looks lovely.'

# Chapter Five

Isabella holds her breath and lies very still, listening. She thought she heard a sound, but she cannot be sure since she was crying so hard. Now her head hurts more than her body. Yet the mere thought of a cane makes her wince; the memory of the pain it inflicted is still excruciatingly vivid. It is as though she stepped out of a fire, but the terrible blaze is still there, just a breath away from her body, ready to consume her, for Lady Wulvedon can have her punished whenever the mood strikes her.

She could never have imagined such agony was possible. Only a few hours ago *severe* and *punishment* were merely two words. She imagined she could filter their meaning through her mind and lessen their impact, but their reality was so intense she was able to grasp it only with her flesh, and now nothing will ever be the same again. She never truly realized before how vulnerable she is. She had not become aware of her body as a vitally important part of what makes her who she is until she arrived at the Castle. Growing up surrounded by books, she believed her personality was essentially the sum of her thoughts, which conceptually defined the boundaries of her self, and that physical needs such as eating and sleeping and staying warm had nothing to do with who she was, not really.

The cane's inexorable statements have made it clear to Isabella that she is literally much more than she thought she was – because she can experience feelings defying comprehension – and yet also much less. Now she knows what *severe punishment* is, she will bite her tongue and endure that minor discomfort and frustration before she ever talks back at Lady Wulvedon again and willingly suffers the cane's brutal despair. And this profoundly humiliating knowledge is why she has been crying beneath the covers of her luxurious bed since Ludly escorted her back to her room. She was surprised by his strength as he allowed her to lean on him the whole way, although she needed moral support more than anything else. Before they left Lady Wulvedon's quarters, Rose silently handed her a simple, sleeveless white slip, and the soft material felt wonderfully cool against her smoldering skin. But she shivered from cold during the long walk back through the torch-lit corridors and, already dazed, these further intense contrasts sapped what remained of her strength. She was very grateful when Ludly let her hold on to his hand as she climbed the steps up to her bed, and collapsed facedown across it.

'I will bring your dinner straight away, miss,' he said gently.

'I am not hungry,' she mumbled into the comforting feather-stuffed mattress.

'I will bring you a tray nonetheless, miss.' He left, and returned in what felt like the blink of an eye as she dozed off seeking the peace of unconsciousness undisturbed by a single dream, which all seemed to have been beaten out of her. She barely remembers being taken down from the 'tree'. She was aware only of her immeasurable relief the ordeal was over and that Lady Wulvedon was nowhere in sight. It confused her when Elaine stepped behind her and rested a deliciously cold wet cloth over her flaming bottom for a long moment, before moving it gently down to her throbbing thighs. She could not understand why Elaine and Rose seemed to care about her feelings now.

They had watched another girl beat her nearly senseless without moving a muscle to help her, and yet they gently tended to her wounds afterwards. It made no sense at all, and at the time Isabella did not have the strength to even try to comprehend such behavior. She still does not. She barely has the energy to wonder about the small sound she imagines she just heard in the darkness. She thought she heard the door open. Ludly extinguished nearly all the candles before he left, and the bed's lavender canopy further diffuses the faint, flickering illumination provided by the few remaining flames, which stretch fervent, fiery arms towards her as she blinks tears out of her eyes and sits up.

There is just enough ghostly illumination for her to make out two pairs of broad shoulders blacker than the darkness itself, telling her it is two men who have secretly entered her room. Strangely enough, this strikes her as a good thing because it implies Lady Wulvedon is not behind the sinister intrusion, and the relief the thought fills her with scarcely leaves any room inside her for fear. So she merely sits there with the covers pulled up to her chin as the tall shadows approach the bed.

A man's deep voice asks quietly, 'Isabella?'

The sound of her name gives the darkness a reassuring soul and her heart leaps hopefully in her chest as she replies, 'Yes?'

'Our little teacher is awake,' the second man remarks as he lifts the canopy bed's gauzy veil out of their way.

'What are you doing here?' she whispers.

By way of an answer, they wrest the sheet out of her hands and toss it aside.

She backs up against the pillows, bends her legs against her chest and wraps her arms around them. It is one thing for women to see her in her slip or naked, but these are men… Lord Wulvedon's men! Suddenly, her heart begins beating so hard she is sure they can hear it and know exactly what she is feeling.

The one farthest from her asks, 'Did Bridget punish you?' as he reaches forward, finds her ankles, and drags her casually towards him until her knees bend over the edge of the bed.

'Yes!' she gasps as if pleased by his violent gesture.

The one who said her name grabs a fistful of her slip and pulls her up into a sitting position. 'Was she hard on you?'

'Yes…' She feels as helpless as a doll in their hands, and her mind seems to have gone as strangely blank… she is suddenly aware only of her body, of how easily they can move it and make it do whatever they want it to…

Both men reach down to her ankles and begin raising her nightgown. They caress it gently up her legs, and there is nothing she can do about it since they are also both gripping one of her wrists. 'What did she use on you, Isabella?'

'A cane… please stop,' she begs softly without understanding why, because what they are doing actually feels good, dangerously so…

'How many strokes did you take?'

'I lost count…' She is finding it nearly impossible to think about anything except their warm, heavy hands moving up her thighs.

'Are you a virgin, Isabella?'

'Yes, my lord,' she replies calmly, having used up all her indignation when Lady Wulvedon asked her this question.

His companion steps aside as the man addressing her gently spreads her thighs. 'Do not be afraid, Isabella, just lie back and relax.'

Knowing she has no choice but to obey him makes her feel curiously languid as she falls back across the bed.

'If you hold still, I will not hurt you,' he promises, and slowly dips two of his thick fingers into her body's unplumbed depths.

'Oh, no…' she moans, and yet at the same time is disappointed when he heeds her breathless cry and pulls his fingers out of her tight pussy.

'She is intact,' he states, and lifts her effortlessly up into his arms.

With a small breathless sound, which can in no way be construed as a protest, she slips her own arms around his neck and rests her cheek against his cool leather shoulder.

He carries her across the room, his companion opens the door, and they turn right down the torch-lit corridor. This small detail surprises her, because both times she saw Lord Wulvedon she turned left, and it upsets her into raising her head and shifting anxiously in his arms.

'Where are you taking me?' she enquires as calmly as possible. She has never been so close to a man's face before, except her father's, of course, which may be why she finds it comforting even though his hard expression is not very reassuring.

'You will see,' he answers curtly.

Whenever they pass beneath a torch she is able to make out faint lines at the corners of his eyes and mouth, another reassuring resemblance to her father contributing to how safe she feels in his arms despite the fact that she has no idea where he is taking her or even what he is planning to do with her. She is sure, however, even though he has not actually said so, that Lord Wulvedon sent him, and this fills her with a wonderful sense of hope. The feeling goes straight to her head like wine and suffuses her belly with a delicious, debilitating warmth. She has never experienced anything quite like it before, and it makes her want to keep asking nervous questions even as her deepening excitement tells her there is only one answer defying explanation…

'Are you frightened, Isabella?' the man holding her asks abruptly.

She gazes earnestly up into his face. His cheeks look slightly rough, as though he has not shaved in a day or two, and his well-shaped features help fill all the empty spaces she was aware of inside her when she was alone in her room, crying. 'No, my lord,' she answers truthfully.

The other man slows down and begins walking beside them to study her expression, and whatever he sees dims his smile in a way that makes her wonder if she should not perhaps be just a little concerned.

'Why are you not afraid, Isabella?' He shifts her weight in his arms to position her more comfortably against him. 'Are you accustomed to being abducted by two strange men in the middle of the night?'

'Of course not.' She is sure he is teasing her. 'But since I arrived at the Castle, my lord, so many strange things have happened to me that I am not at all surprised.'

'I did not ask if you were surprised, Isabella, I asked you why you are not afraid.'

They are passing through a shadowy stretch between torches and she cannot see his eyes. 'Should I be afraid?' she queries tentatively.

He does not answer. It seems to take forever before they reach the next torch, and the passionately flickering light comes as even more of a blessing in the darkness when it reveals his smile. It vanishes as he asks, 'Had you ever been beaten before today?'

'No, my lord, never.'

'And did you enjoy it, Isabella?'

'*Enjoy* it? How can you ask such a thing?'

Again he does not reply as his companion pushes open a black, silver-studded door very much like the one leading out into the beautifully spacious courtyard with the fountain. She cannot be sure of the dimensions of the space into which they emerge now, lit only by two torches burning on either side of the largest set of double doors Isabella has ever seen.

Cold stone kisses the soles of her bare feet as Lord Wulvedon's man sets her down abruptly. Reflected tongues of fire lick across the polished black marble floor but do nothing to warm it, and she trembles as a chill travels up her spine and reminds her all she is wearing is a thin white shift.

'Go on in, Isabella.' Her escort gives her a gentle shove as his companion grips a massive wrought iron handle with both hands, and pulls open one of the heavy doors just far enough for her to slip through the crack.

She has no idea what awaits her, yet she does not hesitate to step into the darkness on the other side. The door closes behind her and she looks up to sees stars, countless stars visible through a glass ceiling so far above her it makes the tiny pulsing lights look even more impossibly far away; the vastness of the universe at once enhanced and eclipsed by the monumental manmade space opening up before her. Then by the steady illumination of widely spaced gas lamps she discerns what looks like shelves rising for as far as she can see – shelves filled with books, as many books as there are stars winking down at the library of her dreams.

'Oh, my God,' she whispers. 'Oh, my God!' There appear to be three levels, the main floor she is on, and two more above it accessible by way of black spiral staircases.

Shivering, Isabella hugs her body and smiles with joy to find herself surrounded by undeniable evidence that her faith in Lord Wulvedon was justified, for she had feared this faith might only be her desperate imagination. She expressed to him her fervent wish to see the library, and he promptly granted it. Now she understands why his men came for her in the middle of the night – because Lady Wulvedon must not know about this.

Not only does it not matter to her that she is barefoot, she is almost glad of it since it brings her into unquestionably real contact with what she might otherwise mistake for a dream. The absolute silence is an almost physical pressure against her chest that, combined with her excitement, makes her strangely conscious of her every breath. She walks over to the nearest shelf, and stretches her arms out before her like a sleepwalker to run her fingertips across cool leather spines. She does not attempt to read any titles in the dim light; it is enough for now to sense the boundless wealth of knowledge surrounding her like God's own invisible arms. Closing her eyes, she rests her cheek against one particularly thick spine, and sighs contentedly, as if she is literally being held against a divine chest.

Unfortunately, when her eyes open again she sees things a bit more clearly. Reluctantly, she realizes she will scarcely be able to taste the feast spread out before her. She will not be able to spend hours here every day nourishing her mind since, for some devilish reason of her own, Bridget will not permit it. And suddenly Lord Wulvedon's seemingly noble gesture strikes her as cruel, as though she was foolishly admiring an elegant sword, the point of which she now becomes aware of against her heart; because he is deliberately whetting her appetite and making it even more painfully sharp by allowing her to see what she cannot have. During the day, the sun's rays will pour down into the library across the pages of any open books. At night, a handful of lamps barely provide enough light to make out even the gilded titles, much less small black print.

As Isabella pushes herself away from the shelf in angry frustration, her vision is drawn up towards the second floor. A light is burning above her that is different, brighter and less steady than the soft amber atmosphere cast by the gas lamps, and she immediately feels herself drawn towards it like a delicate moth in her thin white shift. Somehow, she senses a presence in the flickering illumination distinct from the undemanding personalities of the books.

She hurries over to the nearest spiral staircase and starts up the cold metal steps. The ascent seems to take forever as she goes round and round, very much like a dizzy little moth. She considers calling out and asking if anyone is there, but her voice is spellbound by the profound silence.

When she at last makes it to the second floor, she takes her courage in hand and steps around a bookshelf into the warm glow.

Her eyes alight on two black soles resting on a wooden table next to a black wrought iron candelabra holding a dozen burning red candles. The black boots lead her down a long path of slender legs in black leather leggings to the pages of an open book, and from there she moves quickly up to a man's face gazing back at her. A black goatee frames his thin mouth and his eyes are impenetrably dark, yet his smile is as soft as his features are sharp.

'Good evening, again.' Lord Wulvedon closes the heavy tome resting on his lap with a thud that makes her jump. 'Or rather, *good morning*, Isabella.'

'Good morning, my lord.' She quickly crosses her arms over her chest to hide her breasts. She had not noticed her firm nipples nearly poking through her shift until she felt his eyes on them.

He slides his boots off the wooden table, sets the book down and rises, all in one smooth cat-like motion. 'Are you cold, Isabella?'

'Yes, my lord.' She backs away from him.

Her tense little steps are no match for his long, relaxed strides. 'Come here.' He grasps one of her wrists gently and leads her back over to the table. 'Show me your marks.'

'But… but my lord,' she gasps, 'I cannot possibly—'

'Lean forward and put your hands on the table, Isabella.'

She remembers what his sister said about him as she suddenly feels like a rabbit squirming in the calmly unrelenting jaws of a wolf. Instinctively, she knows if she makes a futile effort to get away it will only make things worse for her in the end, so she obeys him. She leans forward and rests her hands on the table, lowering her head in shame at what she is about to let him do, grateful for her long hair, which falls forward around her face to hide her hot cheeks.

'Good girl. You only arrived a few days ago? You learn quickly.'

'Yes, my lord,' she whispers.

'What is wrong, Isabella? You had no problem speaking up earlier when you rudely yelled out my name, and then shamelessly introduced yourself to me in front of my men.'

For the second time in one night she feels a man's hands raising her nightgown, only Lord Wulvedon does not stroke it slowly up her legs; he pulls the hem swiftly up to her waist and exposes her bottom. Yet it is the tone of his voice and what he said, not the feel of his hands caressing her tender cheeks, that makes her whimper in distress. He did not seem offended at the time, and her confusion only deepens when her humiliation begins battling another very different feeling as his firm hands move slowly down to her thighs.

'Beautiful,' he murmurs. 'Beautiful…'

Her head starts spinning in a way that is becoming all too familiar. She cannot possibly suddenly be glad of ugly welts or of the terrible beating responsible for them merely because they seem to please him; merely because his deeply appreciative voice flows through her blood like drugged wine. It is not natural how weak his voice makes her feel…

'Do they hurt?' he asks gently or indifferently, she cannot be sure which.

'Only a little, my lord.' She makes an effort to speak in her normal voice as she reluctantly becomes aware of his hands moving slowly back up to her buttocks, making another part of her ache in a strange way. Her legs are spread just far enough apart to offer him a clear view of the private space between her thighs she has never seen herself, and her pussy is growing warmer and warmer as if with shame at being so wantonly exposed.

'Are you afraid of pain, Isabella?'

'Yes,' she says fervently.

'Why?'

'Because it is like standing in fire, my lord…' Even though the answer seems obvious, she nevertheless strives to put into words for him what she felt as she was being caned. 'My soul feels as though it wants to burn right through my flesh!'

'Because it desires to escape?'

'No, my lord,' she has to think about it a moment before

concluding, 'it is my body that is desperate to get away from the torment.'

'Excellent, Isabella, you are close to grasping the secret after only one beating. I am impressed.'

'*Secret*, my lord?' she asks, and yet the answer is really not as important as how thrilled she is that he is pleased with her.

'The secret, Isabella, is your soul feeds off your body's suffering like the spirit of fire on the destruction of its temporary host, and the whisper of a cane or of a whip or of a riding crop,' his hard forgers suddenly give her buttocks a painful squeeze, 'is the gust of wind bringing it fully to life for a beautiful, blazing moment.'

His sonorous voice almost has her believing pain is a positive thing when she knows perfectly well she does not feel that way about it at all, yet a treacherous part of her is drawn to the seductive picture he paints for her.

'There are many different kinds of pain, Isabella.'

She definitely does not like the sound of that, and anxiety compounds her disappointment when he suddenly lets her nightgown fall to her ankles again. Then she feels him grab a handful of her hair at the back of her head, and winces in real pain as he pulls her up by it.

'You are very tempting,' he whispers in her ear.

'Thank you, my lord,' she replies, just as softly.

'Do not thank me, Isabella.' He tugs on her roots, forcing her head back. 'You are in a very dangerous position.'

His mouth fills her vision, an inscrutable horizon she finds herself longing to touch with hers to explore what lies on the other side, sensing his lips will open up a whole new and excitingly dangerous world. Then she looks up into his eyes. 'Please, my lord,' she whispers without any idea what she is asking him for, until he lets go of her, and then she knows that is not what she wanted.

He pulls a leather chair away from the table and seats himself in it, facing her. 'Kneel before me,' he commands.

Her hand flies up to her chest as her heart starts beating so fast she is afraid she might faint. She sees his boots are planted far enough apart to accommodate her slender figure as she suddenly seems to be in two places at once – there in the library with him and hiding in a dark corridor watching him with another girl. 'I cannot possibly!' she gasps.

'You cannot kneel, Isabella? You must have a difficult time in church.' Swift as a snake his right hand reaches up, grabs the nightgown between her breasts, and yanks her down to her knees before him.

'No, please, my lord, please do not make me!' Her hands fall on his thighs to steady her, but she immediately snatches them away and clasps them anxiously behind her back.

'Make you do what?' he asks patiently.

She cannot even begin to answer that.

'Look at me, Isabella.'

He is so close there is nowhere else she can look without turning her face away, which is not possible because he cups it lightly in his hands like a flower, leaving her no choice but to meet his eyes. 'Make you do what?' he asks again quietly. His eyes are a dark gray-green, the charged slate color of the sky in which a storm is brewing as night falls.

'I have a confession to make, my lord…'

He sits back and rests his hands on his thighs, drawing her gaze down to his sensitive looking fingers as he asks curiously, 'A confession? I am intrigued. Confess away, Isabella, and I shall meet out the proper penance.'

'Only a priest can do that,' she breathes, terrified by the prospect of *severe penance*.

'I *am* a priest,' he replies seriously, 'although I do not expect you to understand yet. Pain speaks with a divine voice, Isabella. What you suffered today was a sacrament. Take that thought to bed with you every night, and now tell me what it is you have to confess.'

'I saw you with Juliet the other day in the corridor, my lord,' she says all in one breath, hanging her head, 'when you were…'

'Go on,' he urges quietly. 'How much did you see and how did it make you feel?'

'I think… I think I saw *everything*, my lord, and I do not understand what I felt, all I know is I have not been able to think about anything else since then.'

'I see.'

She cannot look away from his eyes; she has no desire to. She senses him understanding things about her she cannot comprehend herself, as distinctly as she feels him reaching around for her hands, and then holding them down with both of his over the firm bulge between his legs. His leather pants are cool, but she can detect his warmth through them as a strangely delicious swelling fills her palms.

'Do you wish to serve me, Isabella?'

'Yes, my lord,' she says without hesitation.

'Do you realize the profound honor I am doing you by even asking that question, Isabella?'

'Yes, my lord,' she gazes earnestly into his eyes. 'Thank you.'

'We will have to be careful,' he warns quietly.

'Yes, my lord,' she says a third time, her gaze drawn irresistibly down to the increasingly firm fullness beneath her hands. 'I will do whatever you say.'

'Prove it, Isabella. Before you return to your room tonight, prove to me that you will, in fact, do anything I say no matter how shocking or painful it may be for you. Are you prepared to do this for me?'

She is not, yet she reminds herself this was how she felt when she was six-years-old and her father placed her on top of a big black horse. She grabbed its wild mane and held on for dear life as she gradually learned to ride her fear. 'Yes,' she whispers, 'I am prepared to prove it to you, my lord. Please tell me what to do.'

'Go and bend over the table again, and this time lift your nightgown for me yourself and offer me your lovely bottom. I wish to pierce that wounded little heart.'

She gets up, unable to imagine what he means by this, which is just as well, because not knowing what awaits her makes it mysteriously easier to prepare herself. Yet this was what she thought about severe punishment; she believed she could just get it over with, and suddenly she is so frightened her nightgown and her fingers might as well be made of marble for all the power she has to move them.

Remaining seated, Lord Wulvedon does not say a word while she stands rooted to the spot watching him unbutton his leggings. He does not need to speak; she feels her shift sliding slowly up her legs, lifted by the invisible yet irresistible force of his will. He rises, and she quickly gathers the soft material around her waist, her eyes fixed on his hands holding his leggings closed, the strange hunger she feels waiting for him to reveal himself stronger than her shyness.

'You are dying to see it again, are you not, Isabella?'

It is true she cannot take her eyes off the potent space between his hips from which she saw his long, glistening shaft pouring straight out into a girl's mouth…

'Turn around,' he says harshly.

She is disappointed, but she obeys him at once and bends

submissively over the table. She concentrates on the flickering heat of the candles burning beside her as she feels him step up behind her.

'This is going to hurt very much, Isabella.'

'Oh God,' she moans, for the first time since his death almost hating her father for leaving her so alone and helpless.

'You will feel as though I am killing you,' he warns. 'You will beg me to stop, but I will *not* stop. Do you understand, Isabella?'

'Yes, my lord,' she whispers miserably. It hurts already how roughly his thumbs dig into her flesh as he separates her buttocks. 'What are you going to do?' she begs to know.

He does not answer as she feels something both firm and tender touch her bottom's tight opening, and then begin pushing into her body from behind.

'Oh!' she cries as what can only be his stiff penis makes the tight little hole between her bottom cheeks start screaming silently open around it. She cannot believe it, yet it is undoubtedly happening – he is forcing his erection into a part of her she never dreamed could be so invaded. She closes her eyes, whimpering in growing pain as he forces her to accept the impossible. Then he groans deep in his throat, and the knowledge she is pleasing him falls cool and deep as a shadow over the blinding torment. For some reason, his appreciation soothes her discomfort enough for her to admit to herself that even though what he is doing is profoundly disturbing, she much prefers the punishment of his hard cock stabbing her to being caned. He makes another sound of pleasure she echoes with a helpless cry, feeling herself stuffed alive and yet surviving. But she has to bite her lip in order not to scream as his excruciatingly large erection impales her, and then begins moving in and out of her virginal bottom with swift carving strokes she is afraid will split her right open in his hands.

'Oh my lord, please stop, I cannot bear it!' she cries. 'I cannot bear it!'

But he does not stop, as he said he would not, so she finally ceases begging him to and simply gasps every time he thrusts deep, only to pull his breathtakingly hard length back out and stab her with it again, and again. The ordeal seems to go on forever, the sensations so intense she fears they will kill her, and yet she mysteriously survives every time. She recognizes the relentless rhythm that hypnotized her as she watched another girl's mouth taking it, and finds herself desperately clinging to the memory of how it made her feel…

'Mm, Isabella, you are delicious!'

'Oh my lord, *please*…' It stuns her every time his firm body kisses the soft cheeks of her bottom in the overwhelming instant he rams himself all the way inside her, the feel of his cool testicles slapping against her warm pussy her only comfort. The subtle sensation strikes her as the promising whisper of an angel in the depths of hell, and concentrating on it gradually and miraculously dims the hot suffering of his penetrations to a purgatorial ache. Yet at the same time she feels as though he is opening her body up dangerously as he drives into her faster and harder…

He lets out a sound like a growl and yanks her hips fiercely against him.

'Oh God!' she sobs, suddenly so full of him she knows she is going to die, but then she is amazed to feel his penis pulsing inside her like a second heart, mysteriously sustaining her while flooding her with an exquisite sense of fulfillment more powerful even than the pain.

# Chapter Six

Isabella moans, and attempts to burrow into the mattress, squirming in defiance of the growing illumination beating gently against her eyelids. She buries her face in the pillow and folds its thousands of feathers up around her head, refusing to land in reality yet. She struggles to hold on to sleep's all-numbing darkness, but it is wearing off and her soul is beginning to feel the ache of what she does not wish to face, which this morning happens to be life itself.

Finally, a slow, repetitive shuffling noise inspires her to raise her head in order to discern its source and find a suitable object to throw at it, for the sound scratches annoyingly at her mind and she is trying not to let any thoughts in at all.

Through the violet mist of the canopy, she discerns Ludly dragging his slightly stooped frame slowly from scone to scone. He is lighting the humble little candles acting as the servants of the all-powerful sun welcoming her to a new day, whether she likes it or not.

'Stop, that is enough light,' she says brusquely, and then she feels guilty. 'Thank you, Ludly.'

'Good afternoon, miss.'

'Afternoon?' She sits up. 'Did you say *afternoon*, Ludly?' Panic sparks in her mind, stoked by confusion, because she cannot believe Lady Wulvedon let her sleep through her lesson. If she did it was certainly not out of kindness, but because it would provide her with another very good excuse to punish her severely.

'Yes, miss, three o'clock in the afternoon, to be precise.'

'Oh, my God.' She collapses across the pillows and stares up in horror at the dark heaven of the canopy. 'That is not possible!'

'Lady Wulvedon said not to wake you, miss, as she would not be taking any lessons today. She and the master are out hunting. Winter will soon return with a vengeance and they wished to take advantage of the lovely weather.'

Isabella suffers the queer impression her emotions are a litter of newborn kittens nesting in her chest when they begin clawing at her blindly whilst trying to find their legs. An intense relief wars with an equally powerful resentment that suddenly has the blood pumping swiftly through her heart. The beautiful Lady Wulvedon and her handsome dark-haired brother are out hunting today. This means she can relax for a while. She should be happy, but instead a jealousy so sharp it seems to puncture a hole in her lungs makes it hard for her to breathe. She is condemned to the cloying smell of burning wax and to frigid shadows while they are out enjoying the fresh, crisp air and the soft brilliance of the winter sun. Yesterday *she* was the stupid, helpless creature caught in their seductive traps. Today it is a fox, or perhaps a lovely deer, they are after.

She throws off the covers, crawls to the edge of the bed and hurries lightly and purposefully down the steps. 'Ludly, you must help me get away,' she says firmly.

'Miss?'

She opens her black trunk and begins throwing dresses into it carelessly. 'You must help me get away, Ludly.' She picks up some books and arranges them carefully over the dresses.

'Might I ask,' he clears his throat as though her request is sticking in it like a chicken bone, 'where you intend to go, miss?'

89

'Anywhere. It does not matter. I simply have to get out of here.'

He clears his throat again, and she glances at him surprised he could produce such a strong sound. 'Miss, Lady Wulvedon wishes me to inform you that you will be dining with her tonight.'

'Oh no…' She will never be able to close the trunk; her wadded up dresses are taking up too much room and she forgot to leave one out she could wear for the journey.

'Lord Wulvedon requests the honor of his sister's company,' Ludly continues placidly, 'and of her new tutor's, at his table this evening.'

A small stack of books slips out of her nerveless fingers onto the woven forest beneath her feet, their old brown leather covers merging with dark tree trunks as though returning home. 'I am to dine with Lord Wulvedon tonight?' She turns slowly around to face the old servant.

'Yes, miss, and I have brought what Lady Wulvedon wishes you to wear.'

Isabella follows his gaze to a chair, where she sees a gown's lifeless body lying across its stiff arms. She moves towards it suspiciously, yet it looks lovely, and she cannot help but be happy her employers are finally treating her with a modicum of respect.

'I also brought you some lunch, miss.' He heads for the door. 'One of Lord Wulvedon's men will come for you later.'

'*When* later?'

'Just be ready, miss.' The door closes heavily behind him.

Isabella gently lifts the gown out of the chair's arms and holds it up before her, frowning. She does not want to be so pleased by it, she does not want to like it so much, but the truth is she is and she does. Apparently,

Bridget actually intends to provide her with a whole new wardrobe, and if this particular dress is any sign of what is to come… it will take her at least six months to work off each one on her current salary, because she cannot possibly accept such expensive gifts without compromising her independence…

Isabella abruptly sinks into the chair, clutching the soft, sky-blue material to her chest as she stares fixedly into space.

The position she finds herself in is like a star burning in the darkness of her inability to comprehend it. It is at once painfully sharp and intensely beautiful, distressingly different from her previous existence yet hauntingly full of promise, its laws cold and detached but also hot and passionate. She cannot quite believe it is real. Everything happening to her, even how she feels about it, is mysteriously beyond her grasp.

Strangely enough, admitting how helpless she is in the face of her new life comforts her, and the momentary peace it affords her allows her to see things as clearly as her inexperience permits. She sits there for a long time, the beautiful gown clutched against her heart, as the invisible threads of her thoughts and emotions weave themselves into some sort of cocooning conclusion she can hold on to. Her blind, destructive urge to run away – because she would not get very far without any money or references – metamorphoses into a determination to make the best of her circumstances, and not only to survive them, but to thrive on them. All she has to do is accept the fact that her life is no longer her own.

It never truly was, she realizes this now. She did not mean to kill her mother when she was born, and yet she did. She did not decide who her father would be, she just got lucky, and in the end she could not stop him from leaving her. She did not choose to be born a girl with brown hair and eyes. Her life now, as always, is in God's hands… and in Lord and Lady Wulvedon's.

'No,' she says out loud as her reflections all listen attentively. 'I am in God's hands alone. If someone has power over me it is because, for some mysterious reason, God has granted them that power for my own good. It may not seem that way, or especially *feel* that way, sometimes, but in the end there is a divine purpose behind everything, I just know it!'

Her large eyes focus on her surroundings again, and alight on the tray of food Ludly brought her. Seeing it, she realizes she is absolutely starving. She was in no mood to eat her dinner yesterday after being beaten for the first time in her life, and she slept right through breakfast.

She gets up and drapes the gown gently over the back of the chair, her gaze lingering on its delicate, almost magically seamless, length. Lord Wulvedon will see her in this tonight… her belly growls with hunger as another much more intense feeling flashes through her womb. She quickly sits down at the table, rips into a hunk of moist black bread, and refuses to think about Lord Wulvedon. She cannot let herself think about him, not yet. If she starts thinking about him, and what he did to her last night, she will not be able to eat and she needs her strength. Yet in her mind's eye she is seeing his lean figure dressed all in gleaming black… she moans and washes down the piece of bread stuck in her throat with half a glass of wine.

If it was not for the dull ache in her bottom, she might almost be able to convince herself she dreamed that magnificent library, and everything else. Oddly enough, she is glad of this physical evidence what happened between her and Lord Wulvedon was real, and suddenly his deep voice flows through her memory so clearly she actually seems to hear it in the room with her. 'Do you wish to serve me, Isabella?'

She catches sight of her face in a mirror, and turning her head, she sees another one of her selves gazing back at her from a slightly different angle. It must have been one of *these* Isabella's who answered him so passionately and so shamelessly.

Instead of windows opening out onto the world, she sees only herself now everywhere. Yet, paradoxically, every day she is less and less certain of who she is, even of who she was, never mind who she will be, if she survives.

On the growling insistence of her stomach she picks up a hunk of yellow cheese and bites into it, but then she makes the mistake of remembering what it felt like when Lord Wulvedon pulled the cheeks of her bottom apart...

She reaches for the wine again.

Isabella is still wondering what to do with her hair when Lord Wulvedon's man arrives. He does not bother to knock, and he makes scarcely a sound entering the room, so when he abruptly appears behind her in the mirror she lets out a little yelp and the hair she is artfully arranging on top of her head tumbles down her back.

He laughs, moves up tightly behind her, and smoothes her hair away from her face with both hands. 'You are beautiful, Isabella.'

Speechless, she recognizes him in the glass as the man who had carried her all the way to the library last night.

'Do you have a blue ribbon?' he asks.

She shakes her head, wide-eyed.

'If you did, you could keep your hair out of your face and down at the same time, but since you do not have a ribbon,' he lets her dark locks fall wildly over her shoulders and breasts, 'the wood nymph look will have to do.'

Her heart still racing from the shock of his sudden appearance, she wishes his hard body was not pressing against her soft bottom and reminding her of sensations too intense for comfort.

His hands fall gently to her hips. 'Are you ready, Isabella?'

She nods fervently. 'And I can walk, too.'

He smiles. 'As you wish.'

On the way to the dining room, she once more neglects to mark the twists and turns in the passages she is so busy trying to get a hold of herself, a task made even more difficult by the fact that she scarcely recognized herself in the mirrors. The dress Lady Wulvedon gave her to wear seems to have been made especially for her. It clings to her upper body, the light-blue cloth veined with fine green vines bursting tiny blood-red flowers over her breasts and around her hips in a belt-like decoration. The ankle-length skirt is fuller than it looks and gives her legs room to move, and the long sleeves and high scoop neck keep her warm. When she shivers, it is from an attack of nerves.

When she and her silent escort step out of the torch-lit corridors into the courtyard where she so boldly introduced herself to Lord Wulvedon, she takes a deep, steadying breath of the open air, which tastes even more delightfully refreshing as a result of the live fountain in its center.

Lord Wulvedon's man leads her towards the west side of the rotunda, and up to one of the many black doors. 'Here we are,' he announces.

In the dining room, Lord and Lady Wulvedon are already seated at opposite ends of the long table. The other high-backed burgundy leather chairs are empty, and there is only one other place set at the center of the table exactly between brother and sister. A massive black wrought iron chandelier burning a church-full of candles hangs high above the table from a beam in the Cathedral style ceiling, which is lost in shadow. The soft glow of hundreds of pulsing lights sparkle on exquisite crystal wineglasses reflecting each flame dozens of times over. The black plates, however, selfishly absorb the passionate illumination, making them nearly invisible against the dark-red tablecloth. Beautifully polished silverware rests on snow-white napkins, and the center of the table is a dream-like landscape of wealth and plenty – wine bottles, narrow black vases filled to bursting with colorful wildflowers, and covered silver platters of all sizes that make Isabella wish she and her appetite were getting along better. Finally, the largest fireplace she has ever seen blazes with flames far enough away from the diners the noise of their wild hunger will not interfere with the more civilized feast.

'There you are.' Bridget smiles over at her. 'Come here and let me look at you, my dear.'

Isabella does not dare to even glance at Lord Wulvedon, but she is intensely aware of him in the corner of her eye. It surprises her he is wearing a white shirt, and his mere presence affects her in such a way she finds herself having to concentrate on the heretofore unconscious task of breathing and walking at the same time. She stares fixedly at Bridget's face, which is nothing more than beautiful, as in her mind she hears her brother's deep voice saying 'We will have to be careful'…

'Oh Isabella, you look radiant,' Bridget declares. 'Now tell me the truth, does not fine linen feel much better against your skin than coarse wool?'

'Yes, mistress, much better, thank you.'

Lady Wulvedon's eyes sparkle and some special secret seems about to burst from her smiling lips, but all she says is, 'Bernard, I would like you to meet Isabella, my new tutor.'

'Good evening, Isabella, it is a pleasure to make your acquaintance.'

Her body turns gratefully in the direction it has been longing to go since she entered the room. 'Good evening, my lord, I am honored by your invitation.'

'Take your place between us, Isabella,' Bridget instructs, 'so you may serve us both tasty morsels of your wit during dinner. But first, a small appetizer.'

Her back to the fireplace, Isabella pulls the heavy chair out for herself, and practically falls into it when she sees what Lady Wulvedon considers an 'appetizer' walking slowly out of the shadows.

Rose is wearing only her wildly curling waist-length red hair, and even this is held revealingly away from her face by a loose black ribbon.

Her hot cheeks mimicking the other girl's coloring, Isabella glances at Lord Wulvedon – she cannot even begin to think of him familiarly as Bernard – and is both surprised and thrilled to catch him smiling softly at her instead of looking at Rose, as she does again herself quickly, not knowing which sight is worse since they both have an intensely embarrassing effect on her.

The only thing covering any part of Rose's pale skin are the black-gloved fingers of two of Lord Wulvedon's men as they lead her over to a black rope Isabella abruptly notices hanging from a beam in the ceiling a few feet away from the table. Yet Rose is not resisting. On the contrary, she raises her arms quite willingly, and stares calmly into space as one of the men wraps the rope several times around her delicate wrists. The other man steps away to one side so he is facing her without blocking the table's view of her slender body, which is now stretched taut, forcing her to stand on tiptoe.

It cannot be a comfortable position, but Isabella does not so much find herself sympathizing with the other girl as admiring what the strain does to her body. With her knees and anklebones extended and barely any of her weight resting on the earth, Rose's legs appear even longer and more slender. Her white skin is drawn so tightly over her ribs they stand out as though carved in marble, but her torso is like no sculpture Isabella has ever seen, for her flesh is clearly much too soft to be unfeeling stone, and her rosy nipples look very much alive and sensitive crowning the meltingly tender mounds of her breasts. She is so thin her belly evokes a sunken winter valley above the cool fire of her bush.

'Your expression at this moment is absolutely priceless, Isabella,' Bridget observes. This evening, Lady Wulvedon's bodice looks made of chain mail, although surely it is only designed to resemble armor, and she is wearing a matching ribbon holding her hair back away from her face while allowing it to flow freely down her back.

'Please, share your thoughts with us, Isabella,' Lord Wulvedon requests.

No matter where she looks, she sees something totally arresting. The dining room itself might be a large dark gem enthralling her with all its beautiful facets, and his black goatee is the frame in which it is all mysteriously set for her. His thin lips are like a cut across her mind stretching all the way down to her heart so she cannot tell the difference between thinking and feeling, which prompts her to ask foolishly, 'My thoughts, my lord?'

Fortunately, a hissing sound followed by a sharp smack turns all their eyes back to Rose, who took the whip's first cruel lick without a sound. It is Isabella who gasps as she witnesses the sinister red trail it forges across the haunting steps of the girl's ribs.

Lord Wulvedon pours himself some wine. 'Drink, Isabella,' he says in a tone that prompts her hand to jump out of her lap onto the bottle before her. There is no label, which thankfully provides her with a topic of conversation other than the naked girl being whipped before them.

'Does this wine come from your own vineyards, my lord?'

'It does, Isabella, and my sister and I,' he pauses to take a sip, 'wish you to pour yourself a full glass, and then to drink it all at once.'

A protest perches on her tongue, but she promptly swallows it in time with another hissing crack as Rose's moan seems to emanate from her own soul. She concentrates on the dark bottle, but she remains hopelessly aware of the slender body hanging between it and a bouquet of wild flowers.

She has just finished carefully filling her glass when the whip strikes again. A fine red trail burns across Rose's breasts, intersecting with one of her nipples, and the mere thought of what it would feel like to have the cane strike her there makes Isabella down the wine gratefully. It is delicious, not at all acidic and just the right temperature, not too warm and not too cold. It flows effortlessly down her throat and straight into her blood. When she pauses to catch her breath, her glass is half empty. She catches the glance brother and sister give each other across the table, but its possible significance slips away from her as she raises the sparkling crystal to her lips again, closes her eyes, and allows her growing tension to dissolve in another flood of alcohol. She sets the glass down with a little more force than she intends to, and this time is almost grateful for the attention sharpening snap of the whip.

Lord Wulvedon is smiling at her, the same soft smile he wore when she discovered him in the library last night.

'Excellent vintage,' she declares.

'Every human body is a unique vintage as well.' He sits back and gives the 'appetizer' his full attention even as he continues speaking. 'Our veins are the very special vines which produce the mysterious fruit of our feelings and perceptions, and yet,' he pauses to take a contemplative sip, 'it is not until you crush them and lock them up in the dark and let them stew in their own juices that you create something magical.' He gives a slight nod.

His man begins whipping Rose in earnest, and Isabella finds herself totally absorbed in the riveting experience of another girl's pain. Each time the black leather strip slices into Rose's skin she feels it herself in the treacherous space between her thighs, where all the terrible heat of the other girl's agony is becoming hauntingly concentrated. When Rose's breasts quiver beneath an especially cruel blow, Isabella's own lips part as her breath catches with an awful excitement which is only intensified by her shocked empathy. Her eyes widen in response to the bound girl's cries as though discerning something fascinating and somehow liberating in the shadows where she hangs pale as a ray of light growing mysteriously warmer and brighter with intense suffering. And the longer she watches this vicious spectacle without protesting, without yelling at the man to stop, without doing anything to help the other girl at all, the more sinfully hungry her body gets for more.

Isabella holds her breath when Lord Wulvedon's man pauses to run the full length of the whip patiently through a gloved hand before delivering another vicious stroke to Rose's breasts. The girl screams at last and her whole body tenses like an arrow strung on an invisible bow quivering to be released. Then her head falls forward, and it is clear only the rope around her wrists is holding her up.

Isabella finally surges to her feet. 'You killed her!' she exclaims in horror.

'Only with pleasure,' Lord Wulvedon's resonant voice assures her. 'Cut her down, please, Matthew. I am starving.'

'Sit down, Isabella,' Bridget commands, 'and have some more wine.'

She obeys with alacrity, mainly because it seems like an excellent idea.

The man who stood watching from the shadows steps up to Rose's limp form, and Isabella nearly spills wine across the table when he slips a knife out of the sheathe hanging from his belt. But he only uses the large blade to slice through the thick rope from which Rose is suspended as the other man tosses the whip aside, and catches the result of his cruel work in his arms as she falls. She is not dead after all, because her own arms slip around his neck as he lifts her up against him, and she even raises her face to his. Isabella cannot believe it, however, when she lets him kiss her, not politely as if by way of an inadequate apology, but with a concentrated ferocity which takes her own breath away watching. Then he carries her over to the table.

Lord Wulvedon pushes his chair back abruptly just as Isabella raises her wineglass to her lips, and a red tide breaks down her throat as he rises that makes her eyes water and leaves her gasping for air. Yet the sudden flood of alcohol also suffuses her chest and her womb with breathtaking warmth, profoundly relaxing her, and she does not look away as the freshly whipped girl is laid across the table before him. She watches as he raises her legs up around his head, bends over, and buries his face in her pussy.

Isabella does not notice where the other men go and completely forgets about Bridget as the sight of Lord Wulvedon eating a girl alive consumes her like nothing else ever has. She hates and despises him, she is passionately sure about this if about nothing else, but she cannot even think of looking away. Rose's head tosses from side to side on the table as if in fervent denial of what is happening between her legs, and she seems to resist this experience more than she did the whipping, yet the way her back arches as she cries out only delivers her pussy more completely into his mouth.

Isabella cannot take her eyes off the intense cast of Lord Wulvedon's features setting into another girl's body. She grows increasingly desperate to understand why the sight rivets her as it does; she has to understand why she has no desire to look away from the barbaric scene. She begins to feel as though it will kill her if she does not succeed in throwing some cool comprehension over the sensation rising up inside her from the achingly empty space between her own legs. He groans deep in his throat and the hungry, guttural sounds he makes affect her like blows struck demonically from within her very soul, so she cannot even attempt to defend herself. Then suddenly he looks up at her, and the fierce expression sharpening his elegant features fascinates her into totally forgetting to be embarrassed. She meets his eyes boldly, enthralled by the contrast of his neatly trimmed and controlled goatee with the awareness of his own wild hunger penetrating her in his stare. His lips glistening with Rose's sensual juices, she feels his thoughts touching and caressing hers with a dangerous challenge. He smiles at her, and the clean white strength of his teeth takes a mysterious bite out of her mind, as her body responds with a blinding rush of excitement watching him bury his face between the other girl's thighs again.

She cannot see Rose's expression as she lifts her head off the table to observe Lord Wulvedon feasting on her, and she can hardly imagine what the other girl is feeling as he thrusts his tongue hungrily into her sex…

Isabella's gasp of surprise when her chair is suddenly pulled away from the table is drowned out by Rose's cries.

'Allow me,' a man's amused voice says from behind her, and he is much more successful than she was in thrusting his hand between the cool material of her skirt to cradle the hot mound within.

'Stop,' she whimpers, yet her thighs part willingly and she slips lower in the chair. His hard fingers offer her a different kind of support, a much more important and irresistible reinforcement than the cushioned seat, as she watches Lord Wulvedon's dark brow and sharp nose burrow even more fiercely into Rose's defenseless pussy, so that he looks very much like the wolf his sister compared him to devouring a fresh kill. Then he straightens up abruptly and accepts the dagger Matthew hands him.

Rose whimpers when he plants his free hand on her belly, pinning her hips firmly down against the table, and then a long, keening wail rises out of her as he thrusts the hilt of the knife inside her and stabs her with it repeatedly, a hard, determined look on his face.

The divine sensation Isabella experienced staring at herself in the mirror while thinking about him overwhelms her again, only this time it is much more stunning in its intensity as a strong hand strokes her with relentless skill.

'Really, Bernard,' Bridget sighs dramatically, 'you should learn to control yourself in front of guests.'

'Forgive me, sister.' He pulls the knife out of Rose's limp body. 'I do not know what possessed me.' He gives the glistening hilt an appreciative lick, and winks at Isabella.

She gazes back at him utterly dazed, unable to move even though the other man's arm is no longer pinning her down.

Lord Wulvedon tosses Mathew back his weapon, and waits until Rose is lifted gently off the table and carried away before he resumes his seat. His hard mouth shining with a sinfully rich moisture, he seems to read Isabella's mind as he smiles at her again before wiping his lips clean of another girl's juices with the back of his sleeve. 'Our young guest does not seem to have been able to control herself either,' he remarks.

'I told you she was a wicked little thing.' Lady Wulvedon's tone is wholly approving.

'Mm…' His smile deepens.

Isabella sits up straight, desperately attempting to compose herself, yet the effort seems futile since everyone else seems to know her better than she knows herself. She tosses the hair out of her eyes and stares straight into Lord Wulvedon's, begging him to tell her what to think. The indescribable feeling which flooded her entire being for a few timeless moments has turned her mind into an empty chalice waiting to be filled by the heady elixir of his will. There is truly no such thing as an ordinary life, not if her body can experience such real magic, but the laws of this new world she suddenly finds herself in are still beyond her comprehension, and frighten her into pleading silently with him for guidance if not for protection.

His smile dims as though her dark eyes are sucking all the lighthearted feelings out of him with their intense need. 'I want her,' he says quietly.

'Too bad,' Bridget snaps, 'she is mine. I saw her first.'

'She prefers men,' he states bluntly.

'She only thinks she does because she does not know better yet,' Lady Wulvedon argues firmly, 'because she was raised that way, to accept her eventual fate of marriage and childbirth. I will enlighten her.'

'You are wrong, sister.'

'Oh?' she demands suspiciously. 'And what makes you so sure?'

His tone is dismissive. 'It is obvious.'

'Is it? You should have seen her when her lovely face was buried between my legs. Her tongue is as passionate as her heart and as agile and hungry as her mind.'

'Stop,' Isabella begs, staring fixedly at the bouquet of beautiful dying flowers before her.

'Did you lick my sister's pussy, Isabella?'

She clenches her hands in her lap. 'Yes, my lord.'

'Speak up, I did not hear you.'

'Yes, my lord.'

'Look at me when you address me, Isabella.'

Her eyes cling to his again, but then all her feelings stumble miserably when her intuition cannot seem to grasp his thoughts and brace herself on them. She cannot sense what he is thinking; she is no longer sure of the secret bond between them. When he smiles everything is all right for a blessed moment, until he says, 'She is all yours, sister.' Dropping Isabella's eyes indifferently, he lifts the cover off a silver platter. 'And now I am truly hungry.'

# Chapter Seven

Ìsabella wraps a gray wool cloak over the blue dress she wore to dinner and opens the door to her bedroom. She extinguished all the candles behind her. Even if she paused now to look back at her trunk she would not be able to see it, so she does not glance back at everything she is leaving behind. She realizes she has to sacrifice her dresses, shoes, books and journals if she wants to save her soul, therefore, she ignores the stab of pain she experiences as the door closes on her self.

She turns right down the torch-lit corridor, the direction Lady Wulvedon took for their first lesson under the ancient oak. She has no idea if she will be able to find her way out of the Castle, but she will cease to respect herself if she does not try.

Lord Wulvedon does not care about her in the least, he made that humiliatingly clear at dinner. He amused himself with her briefly, and that is all. She was foolish to think he felt any real sympathy and respect for her. It was incredibly naïve of her to trust him so fervently. It was only her desperate imagination their souls touched through, the magically intimate fingertips of their thoughts and his feelings caressed hers with a special understanding, making her an intensely exciting promise. Her father often told her she had a wonderful imagination, and now she understands why his eyes were sad above his indulgent smile.

As she hurries down the twisting passages, it seems quite natural to move from darkness into light and back again. One minute she feels absolutely miserable, and then hope begins warming the cold darkness Lord Wulvedon's indifference plunged her into as she tells herself he was only pretending not to care about her. Her faith in him resurrects beautifully, only to fade again when she can find no real evidence to sustain it. And this intense emotional conflict, combined with how quickly she is walking, makes her heart beating against her chest feel like her soul's clenched fists demanding the universe pay attention to her.

Isabella has no idea what she will do if she manages to find a way out of the Castle. Strangely enough, this seems like a good thing since it will put her entirely in God's hands. The dark roads outside – all of them leading to a world in which she must somehow survive with nothing at all – are the lines of a divine palm, and whichever path she ends up following in order to save her soul by leaving this sinful place will take her where she needs to go.

At long last she comes to the first large silver-studded door leading out of the maze-like passages. She has no idea where it leads, and she does not care. It takes all her strength to press down on the wrought iron latch with both hands and push open the thick wood, but she manages it and enters an open space she does not recognize.

She pauses, unable to believe her eyes. She seems to have taken all the right turns, and the miracle inspires her to slip her right hand out of her cloak and quickly make the sign of the cross. The moonlight streaming in through the floor-length window directly before her is as clear a sign as she could have hoped for, shining pure and gentle as a divine finger pointing the way out for her.

She rushes towards the blessed light, unable to run as silently as she would have liked across the stone tiles. Yet it scarcely matters how much noise she makes since there is not another soul in sight. But the glass of the windows, she discovers, is broken up into small triangular panes. Even if she dares risk the noise of breaking it, she would need to be as small as a cat to slip out of the Castle this way. Then she realizes the diamond shaped panes belong to a pair of doors, which part as if by magic when she touches the curved black iron latch.

'Thank you,' she whispers fervently, and as the doors close behind her again, she pauses to gaze up at a universe filled with stars. Winter has returned full-force and the frigid air comes as a shocking, sobering slap to her body. Suddenly questions begin cutting into the pure elation of escape, and she merely stands there hugging herself beneath the cloak even as she despises herself for hesitating. Then she stiffens when one of the deep shadows to her left begins flowing like black water towards her feet…

The black cat crosses her path, and glances back at her with indifferent golden eyes.

She stares back at it intently. 'What am I going to do?' she whispers, half hoping for a magical *meow* which will give her a clue as to how she can land on her feet in the world if she leaps wildly out of Lord and Lady Wulvedon's hands now.

The cat looks past her into the Castle, and flows seamlessly back into the darkness.

Isabella peers anxiously over her shoulder.

The tall silhouette making its way toward her seems to burn itself on her vision as if she looked directly at the sun, so that even as she turns and runs she continues seeing its black ghost everywhere. She could not distinguish the face of the man stalking her, but every fiber of her being recognized Lord Wulvedon; already she does not need to see him clearly to know him.

The bitter December air cuts into her lungs and the darkness seems to do everything in its menacing power to put as many obstacles in her way as possible. The smooth garden path she follows off the stone terrace does not get her very far before giving way to uneven ground, treacherous with roots. The large ancient trees let her pass, but their branches toss the full moon around in a way that makes it nearly impossible for her to establish a sense of direction. Luna's steady luminous gaze becomes a mischievous winking between naked limbs, and Isabella suffers the disturbing impression she is following a less obvious path even deeper into the estate, but she cannot stop now. If she allows herself to be caught she will be severely punished for attempting to escape. And yet… she presses back against a broad trunk to catch her breath… she could say she merely stepped outside for some fresh air because she could not sleep. She will still be punished for leaving her room, she is certain of that, but perhaps not as severely…

She keeps running, not daring to look back, yet there is no escaping the thought haunting her. Lord Wulvedon went to her room! Her flight was prompted by the belief he felt nothing for her. But if he felt nothing for her, then why would he go to her room? Had he read her mind at dinner and seen it in her eyes that she had decided to try and escape tonight? She cannot seem to tell the difference between the roots she trips over and these questions; her heart is beating too fast and hard to let her think straight. Running helps keep her body warm, but how cold her ears and her lips are warn her this is a dangerous illusion. Therefore, when she glimpses the side of a small house at the top of a hill, she hurries towards it. Being forced to hold on to her skirt in order not to trip makes it even more difficult to move quickly over the sloping ground since she cannot use her arms for balance, and gradually she realizes there is something strange about the building. It catches the light beautifully, almost as if the moon is admiring her cold complexion in this earthly mirror of smooth white stone. If her wits were not essentially frozen at the moment, she would understand why she knows she will find no succor in the strangely narrow and windowless house. It is not until she crests the hill that the word she is looking for crashes into her mind, ponderous as its marble reality – mausoleum.

The moon and the trees conspired to lead her straight into the Wulvedon graveyard.

Her lungs are so outraged by the freezing air it hurts when she laughs, perversely elated to find herself surrounded by disembodied souls who no longer need to worry about surviving in the world. She thought she had come upon the small home of some poor farmer who might have been kind enough to offer her shelter, instead she is headed straight for the skeletal arms of another Lord or Lady Wulvedon. The intense irony of this fact uses the sharp cold to fell her willpower. Suddenly, her passionate desire to save her soul transforms into the much simpler, and much more immediately urgent, task of preserving her body. Her feet are so cold she can hardly feel the ground beneath her little white boots anymore. A mausoleum is a form of shelter after all, and she can only pray it will be a little warmer inside the tomb, only one of a handful of similar structures scattered across the grass at the top of the hill.

The black wrought iron gate is not only miraculously unlocked, one side swings loosely open almost as if inviting her in.

The light surprises her. She anticipated an absolute darkness in which she would stand trembling in fear waiting for Lord Wulvedon to find her, so it is a pleasant surprise to have the moon's company as the result of a gap between the walls and the vaulted ceiling. Stars also wink down at this eternal resting place, where a large sarcophagus sits high on a platform in the center.

She is not going to succeed in saving her soul – not tonight. She is going to be forced to give up and return to the Castle's purgatory of severe punishment, where she will be just another damned body.

Admitting defeat, and standing still after running hard, makes her feel so strangely calm, and she wanders curiously up onto the stone platform. The lid of the massive coffin is a carved effigy of two bodies lying side by side. Their clothing immediately makes it apparent one figure is a man and the other a woman, clad in a long gown with full sleeves. The man is wearing a suit of fine chain mail, his gloved hands clenched around the hilt of a long-sword resting down the length of his body, the wide blade covering his sex. Their gray stone faces look remarkably alike, and it is not just their smiling acceptance of death that gives their features such a strikingly similar cast. Either they are brother and sister or the artist was not very good.

Isabella shudders imagining Bernard and Bridget buried together like this. Then a small sound behind her prompts her to wrap her arms around herself beneath her cloak and to hold desperately on to her feelings. Turning around slowly, she stands motionless as another statue, watching the gate leading into the mausoleum creak open again.

Lord Wulvedon enters the crypt. 'Isabella,' he says quietly, and there is just enough moonlight for their eyes to meet across the dark space.

Trapped within the marble walls, his deep voice imbues her name with a mysterious power, enabling her to reply fearlessly, 'My lord,' as though they have merely run into each other on a stroll.

His boots make a hollow sound on the stone as he approaches her. He does not ask her what she is doing here. He does not say anything at all.

'If I am to be punished for running away,' she desperately wishes he would speak, for not knowing what he is thinking frightens her, 'please punish me yourself, my lord. Do not just let someone else do it.'

'Isabella,' he steps onto the platform with her, 'I would appreciate it if you would not tell me what to do.'

'Forgive me, my lord.' She moves behind the heads of the eternally sleeping couple, away from him. The moonlight playing on his black leather vest and leggings makes her even more conscious of his relaxed strength and of how his proud, straight-backed carriage is tempered by his cat-like gait. 'Please do not hurt me,' she whispers, and for the first time dares to say his name, 'Bernard…'

He stares down the length of the stone bodies at her. 'Did I hurt you last night?' he asks quietly.

'Yes…' His features are a black and silver mask, yet she seems to see him more clearly than ever, as if their souls are standing naked before each other in this eternal resting place. 'But that is not what I mean…'

'Come here, Isabella.'

'You told your sister I was all hers!' she exclaims, and stays where she is.

'And I told *you* we would have to be careful.'

Her relief is so intense it makes her feel faint, even as she finds herself unable to resist walking back towards him slowly.

He grabs her by the shoulders and traps her between his body and the coffin.

'I miss my father,' she tells him, enjoying the spectral

illusion of intimacy provided by the ghosts of their breaths meeting.

He gently cups her face in his amazingly warm hands. 'I am sorry,' he whispers, and lowering his head, rests his mouth gently over hers.

His lips are cool and firm, and like the edge of a blade the feel of them cuts her to the quick.

He lets her feel the warmth of her name against her cheek as he breathes, 'Oh Isabella…' Then he steps back abruptly and slips his hands into her cloak. 'Do you want me?'

'Yes,' she whispers.

He unfastens her cloak, lifts it off her shoulders, and lets it fall to the floor. 'Then why were you running away from me?'

'Because I thought you did not really care about me… because I do not wish to be merely another body to you.'

'If that is all you were, Isabella, I would not be here now.'

She trembles. 'I am so cold, my lord.'

'I will warm you up,' he promises. 'Trust me.' He reaches up and grasps a silver key, which opens the glimmering black leather over his chest as he pulls on it, exposing his pale flesh all the way down to his navel.

She slips her hands into his vest gratefully. 'You are so warm, my lord.'

'I had a lot to drink, and you run like a rabbit. I nearly lost you.'

'And you are so smooth and so hard…' Her father's chest had been big and tender and hairy.

'Oh yes, I am very hard.' He grabs one of her wrists, pulls her hand down, and forces her to cradle the firm bulge between his thighs in her open palm as his other arm slips around her shoulders. 'Hard for you, Isabella.'

Her cheek resting on his warm chest and her hand full of his mysterious potency, her eyes close contentedly.

Keeping firm hold of her wrist, he caresses his buried erection with her hand. The friction makes her feel oddly breathless, and a delicious urgency like a flame flickering to life begins licking up between her own legs.

'Take it out,' he urges quietly.

The thought of freeing the powerful shaft of his penis frightens her. Yet the mausoleum is a silent chapel, and it is not so much his hands on her shoulders as a profound desire to worship that brings her to her knees before him. She wants to express her faith in him and to receive confirmation of his feeling for her in return. She is very glad he helps her open his leggings because her fingers are stiff with cold, and she is overwhelmed by the sense of daring to take part in a dark sacrament.

'Do not be afraid, Isabella.' He rests both his hands on her head, very much like a priest blessing her. 'Take it out and give it a kiss.'

She reaches obediently into the tight space of his leggings, finds the firm but tender shape curled up inside them, and lifts it out reverently.

His penis rears straight out at her, serpent-like. 'Kiss it,' he commands. His fingers are entwined as inexorably as ancient roots through her hair, making it impossible for her to look away.

She is morbidly conscious of the decayed man lying in the crypt behind her, and of the woman resting peacefully by his side, as she closes her eyes and kisses the tender rift in the tip of Lord Wulvedon's cock. She means only to rest her lips on it for a second, but he pulls her face closer, forcing her mouth open. 'Mm…' she moans in protest, but there is no resisting the pressure of his hands as his erection slides onto her tongue. The moon seems intensely interested in his pale shaft, for she can see it clearly in the darkness as it glides slowly into her mouth like solid light. He disregards the dangerous barrier of her teeth, which for some reason she is careful to keep out of his way as his smooth length penetrates her otherwise very reluctant orifice. Her eyelashes flutter from the effort she makes not to gag as he gently forces her head back and leans over her, reaching down into her body with his remorseless hardness. She is sure she cannot take it. She closes her eyes as her chest heaves with the urge to be sick when his head rubs against the back of her throat. Then once again in her mind's eye she sees that other girl kneeling in a dark corridor, sees her taking his full length down into her delicate throat, not only without gagging but with her eyes seeming to beg for more, and the profound stab of excitement she experiences deep inside relaxes her jaw in astonishment.

'Oh yes,' he murmurs, 'let me fuck your mouth just for a moment…' He slips out from between her lips with obvious reluctance.

She is breathlessly relieved he allows her to stand up, until she sees moonlight glint off the polished blade in his hand. 'No,' she gasps when he clutches a fistful of her dress, thrusts the dagger into it, and slices the fine material all the way down from her belly to her ankles. 'Lady Wulvedon gave me this dress!' she cries in despair.

'You are in trouble now.' He sheathes the knife, and lifts her up onto the hard edge of the sarcophagus behind her. 'We both are.' He spreads her legs.

She clings to his shoulders while both watching and feeling his cool head disappear into the warm darkness of her flesh. It gives her such pleasure to meet him in this way she does not mind the pain as he forces her legs wider apart, making her aware of a muscle in her inner thighs stretching all the way up inside her to a tight space aching with a need she cannot define.

'You are going to bleed,' he warns.

She shifts her hands up from his shoulders to his neck to get a firmer grip on him, and the column of flesh joining his head with his shoulders feels excitingly related to the other hard part of his body pushing into hers. 'Oh God, it hurts,' she sobs, feeling the tip of his rigid penis hit bottom just as his man's fingers did, and yet at the same time she becomes aware of how much deeper she really is...

'Enjoy it,' he commands, and his quiet intensity is more irresistible than the hot flood of pain as his erection breaches her virgin pussy with a single violent thrust.

'Oh my lord, stop,' she gasps. 'Stop!'

His response is to kiss her so furiously his tongue helps her forget the torment of his cock stabbing her relentlessly. She can feel her inner flesh clenching around him, making her hot hole even more agonizingly tight, but she cannot help resisting his penetrations as the edge of the crypt cuts uncomfortably into her bottom through the fine dress. At the same time, however, there is no denying the thrill she takes in being so absolutely full of him, especially since there is no doubt about his feeling for her now.

'Mm, Isabella, if you are this luscious as a bud imagine what you will be like in full bloom.'

'Oh my lord, will it always hurt so?'

'Does it hurt, Isabella?'

'Oh God, yes!'

'Do not fight it. Flow with the pain and let it bring you to me.'

He kisses her again, and somehow she understands what he means when he explains it to her this way, wordlessly and passionately. His neck, his penis and his tongue are all so very firm she cannot help but be happy they are all hers; that he is letting her brace herself on them and cling selfishly to them. And she begins to feel there is something comforting about his steady strokes despite the torment they cause her. She can depend on them. She can rely on his stiff penis to give her all the mysterious support she needs. All she could feel was a burning discomfort until he began kissing her, now she realizes he is attempting to lead her in this shocking dance, and her body glimpses how wonderful it would be if she could relax and fall into rhythm with him.

'Mm…' His lips smile against hers. 'Mm!'

No matter what Lady Wulvedon does to her, Isabella knows she can never reach into her body like this, and it gives him a frightening power over her that only he can caress her from the inside out in this devastating manner. Because even though she feels it might kill her it hurts so much, she loves the overwhelming moment when he thrusts. The experience is so intense it is impossible to be aware of anything except the excruciating fulfillment of his cock slipping in and out of her smoldering pussy. Then she looks down and sees his penis is dark with what can only be her blood, as if he truly is killing her. But it feels more like he is stabbing her to life as she never imagined it could be, so violent and yet so intensely intimate…

He pulls out of her abruptly.

A rush of blood expresses her body's deep disappointment at his loss, which is assuaged by the wonder of watching his stone-hard penis, cradled in his hand and stained with her life, spurting a ghostly white and lusciously milky stream over her throbbing mound.

# Chapter Eight

Isabella has never seen Lady Wulvedon looking more beautifully regal. Her lavender gown's hip-length, form-fitting bodice is exquisitely textured by a design of interwoven vines embroidered in light-blue thread. The skirt is a luminous violet twilight and the half sleeves are misty veils. This is also the first time she has seen Bridget wearing jewelry – a breathtaking necklace of sapphire flowers accentuates the whiteness of her skin, as do matching earrings and a bracelet. Her long hair is piled up on top of her head in an elaborate spiral as smooth and shiny as a seashell. The only touch marring her elegant, almost ethereal, look is her deep and heavy cleavage.

'My poor dear,' she touches Isabella's hollow-eyed face with her cool fingertips, 'you look exhausted.'

'I could not sleep, my lady.'

'Too much on your mind?'

'Oh yes.'

Laughing softly, Bridget turns away, the rustling of her skirt at once crisply efficient and soothingly sensual. 'Well, then,' she sinks gracefully into what appears to be her favorite chair in Isabella's room, 'what am I to learn today?'

'You look so beautiful, my lady.'

'Why, thank you.' Bridget's tone is light, but the almost shy way she glances down at her bracelet seems to indicate she is more pleased by the impulsive compliment than she cares to admit, and this evidence of vulnerability to her opinion amazes Isabella. More than ever, she wishes she could have stayed in bed this morning, safely cocooned in dreams and soft white sheets. Because all she can think about is what Bridget *cannot* learn today or any other day – that Isabella lost her virginity to her brother last night.

'I am sorry, my lady, but I did not have the opportunity to prepare a lesson.' She wrings her hands and looks over at her books, which she lined up in neat rows on a table after unpacking her trunk again, mentally fishing for an interesting subject to feed her student. But nothing seems interesting compared with last night, which was so intense it overflows her ability to remember it clearly. What happened keeps coming back to her in vivid flashes that kick her in the womb and make their way up to her head from there, where what she sees leaves her feeling even more dazed.

'Isabella,' Lady Wulvedon says sharply, 'do you admit to neglecting your duties?'

'Oh no.' Her stomach clenches around an unsettling emptiness; she did not have time to eat breakfast. 'I simply thought I would leave it up to you today, what you wish to pursue in more depth,' she improvises. 'We have touched upon history and philosophy, science and literature, all subjects in which you clearly have a more than adequate foundation. Now we need to determine how deeply you wish to delve into each one.'

Bridget's smile returns with all the threatening moodiness of a cat's swishing tail. 'Very pretty speech, Isabella.' She touches the sapphire flowers around her neck as if enjoying the cold kiss of the precious stones against her skin. 'It was such a lovely little fabrication, I will pretend not to notice you are daring to lie to me, which is a grave mistake.'

Isabella's breath catches even as she tells herself it was merely an unfortunate choice of words. She is seeing the ghost of her own guilt everywhere. 'My lady?'

'Yes?'

She closes her eyes. 'May I visit the library?'

'Well, you certainly are an *insolent* little thing this morning. What *has* gotten into you, Isabella?'

'I told you I would ask you that every day, my lady,' she opens her eyes and walks over to her neat and steadying row of books, 'until you said yes.'

'And your willfulness delights me since I will have to punish you for it.'

The side of the table makes her remember how the edge of the crypt felt against her bottom cheeks through the fine dress, the torn remains of which are lying hidden at the bottom of her locked trunk. It is only a matter of time, however, before Lady Wulvedon finds out her gift was ruined, and notices that the rip in the skirt is much too smooth to be accidental. It was clearly made by a sharp knife, a fact that will give rise to all sorts of questions, none of which Isabella will be able to answer.

She snatches a book at random, walks over to a chair, seats herself, and allows it to fall open across her lap. Everything she does, everything she touches and that touches her, reminds her of the indelible fact that she is no longer a virgin. She was never so acutely aware of objects and textures and of her body's place amongst them as she is this morning.

Afraid Lord Wulvedon's sister noticed her wince as she sat down she clears her throat, and states with as much enthusiasm as she can muster, 'I think today we will discuss the philosophy of symbolism.' Her choice of topics is determined by the heavy book making her distractingly conscious of her thighs, and of how their tender insides are still subtly throbbing from being spread wide open, is entitled *'An Illustrated Encyclopedia of Traditional Symbols'*.**

119

Bridget raises her right hand idly in front of her face to admire her bracelet, and waits.

'Shall we look up *jewels*, my lady?'

'Oh yes, please do.' She adjusts her skirt beneath her, shifting into a more comfortable position. 'I love all my jewels so.'

Isabella refrains from mentioning that Bridget's necklace alone is probably worth more than a few years of her teacher's wages, but the injustice prompts her to flip through the book more passionately than is good for the delicate old paper. '*Jewels*,' she announces, and begins reading the text out loud. '*Jewels symbolize hidden treasures of knowledge or truth... the cutting and shaping of precious stones signifies the soul shaped from the rough, irregular, dark stone into the gem, regular in shape and reflecting divine light... possessing the gem is equated with realization. Sapphire, truth, heavenly virtues, celestial contemplation, chastity.*' She looks up.

Bridget is staring past her as though someone just walked into the room and she cannot decide whether to acknowledge their unexpected presence or to ignore them. 'Yet another interesting book,' she remarks. 'I wonder if we have a copy in our library?'

Isabella meets her eyes. 'I would be happy to check for you, my lady.'

She laughs. 'You are deliciously cheeky this morning.' She cocks her head to one side and runs a teasing finger up one of the chair's dark, heavy arms. 'My brother was quite taken with you.'

Isabella swallows a sudden lump in her throat, remembering the full moon tossed around by the trees she chased all the way to the graveyard, where Lord Wulvedon buried her innocence forever.

'Well, read me another one. Tell me what it says about

*dagger.*'

She scarcely notices flipping back to the appropriate page as she recalls the moonlit blade in his hand slicing down through her skirt… '*Dagger, like the sword,*' she begins breathlessly, '*power, authority… the masculine principle, the active force, phallic, with the sheath as the receptive feminine.*'

'You enjoyed watching Rose being whipped, did you not, Isabella?'

She wants to cry 'No!' but recalling how she felt watching the black leather whip lick the girl's delicate, flushing skin, she hesitates, and then it is too late to deny it.

'Would you like to be whipped, Isabella, while my brother watches?'

Once again the indignation surging through her finds no outlet in a vocal denial. Of course she does not want to be whipped. Of course she has no desire to experience such excruciating pain. 'No,' she says finally, and the lack of conviction in her voice astonishes and frightens her.

Lady Wulvedon rises gracefully. 'I allow him to play with her because Rose is a good girl.' She walks over to a mirror and smiles at her reflection. 'If you learn to be a good girl, Isabella,' she needlessly adjusts one of the pins expertly concealed in her glossy hair, 'if you serve me well and please me as I know you can,' she turns to face her again, 'I will let Bernard play with you, too, every now and then. Would you like that?'

Isabella closes the book and rises with it clutched to her breasts like a shield. 'I do not wish to share your brother with anyone!'

'Oh, my dear,' Bridget's smile is a cruel contrast to her melancholy tone, 'do you have any idea how many lovely young women just like yourself live only to serve Lord Wulvedon?'

'I am not like them,' she declares with all the fierce conviction of absolute despair.

'Of course you are not.' Bridget descends upon her in a wave of silk and satin. 'You are very special, Isabella.' She pries the book out of her hands and sets it down on the table. 'That is why I wish to protect you, not from my brother, who always respects my wishes,' she takes Isabella's rigid body in her strong, slender arms, 'but from yourself.' She strokes her dark hair, which is not imprisoned in a braid today. 'I want to show you that there are other options in life, my dear, other roads we can take society does its best to conceal from women. I simply want to give you the chance to discover whether or not what you have been taught to think and to expect, if what you have been conditioned to believe, is what you truly feel deep inside and what you truly desire. All I ask is that you give me a chance to enlighten you without resisting me, Isabella. And if, after a prearranged amount of time, you still wish to serve my brother instead of me, then I promise I will set you free. Even if what you wish is to leave us, I will see to it you are generously compensated for your time and effort, as well as given excellent references that will help you secure a position elsewhere. You have my word on that as a lady. Trust me, I want only what is best for you.'

The offer of freedom stuns Isabella. It makes her feel as though her heartbeat has turned violently against her soul, because she does not wish to leave now, not after last night. If Bridget thinks she is special, then perhaps Bernard really does, too. On the other hand, they might both just be telling her that, feeding her vanity and her illusion of uniqueness to more easily manipulate her and bend her to their will. Or it might not be so sinister at all, and they merely enjoy toying with her because she makes it so easy for them with her stubborn conceit that what she wants really matters in the vast scheme of things. Yet she cannot discount the possibility Bridget is sincere, in which case she would be foolish to turn down an opportunity to broaden her emotional horizons. Her father always told her that the more you knew the more you came to understand how little you knew, and if you did not feel that way you did not truly know anything.

'My lady,' she says at last, wriggling gently but determinedly out of Bridget's grasp, 'your kindness and concern for my well being mean more to me than I can express.' She pauses, remembering the agony of the cane slicing into her bottom. 'I will seriously consider your offer, if I might have forty-eight hours to do so, please.'

Isabella can think or do nothing to assuage her state of profound agitation. It is like nothing she has ever felt before, like most everything she has felt since arriving at the Castle. And it is not just an emotional restlessness; she feels as though her pulse is out of control. Yet when she rests two fingertips on the gentle beat in her throat, the slow, calm rhythm mocks her anxiety. She is definitely short of breath, however. As if her lungs are still in shock from her rash foray into a frigid December night, they cannot seem to take in as much of her bedroom's warm, wax-scented air as usual. Perhaps that is why she feels so strangely lightheaded, and why she catches herself taking quick, heady breaths through her mouth as she keeps reliving last night in debilitating flashes.

She has approximately forty hours left to give Lady Wulvedon her answer, for at least eight hours have passed since she was left alone in her room again, and she cannot help but wonder what Bridget will do if she says no.

What was she hoping, that Lord Wulvedon would request the honor of her company at his table again, this time alone? That he would send her a secret message by way of one of his men? Well, neither of these things has happened. Ludly shuffled in with her dinner tray, and shuffled back out again, a very long time ago. She is officially at war with her appetite now, but painful hunger pangs forced her to bite into some rosemary-perfumed bread and into a little grilled bird she could not identify, both of which she washed down with a good amount of the Castle's delicious red wine. Now she is sitting desultorily in a chair next to the hourglass, chin in hand watching the flesh-colored sand flow smoothly and silently down from one chamber into the other… life's endless flow of seconds all running into each other… the past is only a memory, the future is always a dream, and the present is eternally trapped between them in what, at least at the moment, is a very frustrating way.

She is nearly down to thirty-nine hours… Lord Wulvedon has approximately thirty-nine hours to declare his love for her, thirty-nine hours to defy his sister and go against his own pleasure loving, promiscuous nature…

She gets up abruptly and walks over to the nearest mirror. 'You are a fool,' she tells her reflection, 'a complete and utter fool.' Yet at least she is a lovely fool. Lord Wulvedon's man told her she was beautiful, and he himself complimented her looks simply by focusing his attention on her so thoroughly. Her profound self-confidence is blossoming into a visceral awareness of how attractive she is as it dawns on her what a vital part what she looks like is playing in her life. Staring at herself now she feels rather foolish, like a child who has cut and bloodied her hands on a knife because she did not realize it could hurt her. Staring straight into her own darkly glimmering eyes, Isabella grasps the strangely dangerous fact of her beauty. Suddenly, she understands the emotional and sensual wounds she has suffered lately are a direct result of her beauty, and becoming conscious of this fact is like grasping the knife by the hilt. She can learn to use her looks to her advantage. She can also learn to defend herself with them somehow and, if necessary, she can learn to use them to get what she wants. After all, she has only herself to rely on now. All the mirrors surrounding her focus her determination in a way simply dwelling on the thoughts and feelings churning inside her cannot. Her lovely reflections encourage her to stop looking at things from the inside out and to start seeing them from the outside in, the way other people see her, which might help her ascertain what they are thinking and what their intentions really are.

She frowns and turns away from the pane as something else it tells her quite clearly darkens her hopes with despair. She is just another pretty girl. Lord Wulvedon cannot see her soul. He does not know her as she knows herself or as her father knew her. The things she says, the expressions on her face, the look in her eyes, all hint at the intensity of her nature, but these clues take time to perceive and process and she needs to blind him with her beauty so he no longer sees the differences in their social status, so he no longer sees Juliet or any of the other girls who live only to serve him.

She plants both hands on her temples and squeezes her eyes shut. The thought that she means nothing to Lord Wulvedon at all keeps thrusting like a hot poker through her brain. Even the pain she felt when her father died was not as terrible as this. She missed him and longed for his company, but her grief was, she realizes now, soothed by the sense of his love still mysteriously surrounding her. Not even the agony of the cane slicing into her skin was as bad as this torment of Lord Wulvedon's indifference after she gave him the irreplaceable gift of her virginity. She can never get it back to offer another man, it is his forever, and it obviously means nothing to him.

Her eyes open and alight on the little laughing Buddha.

She snatches up the statuette, raising her arm to fling it across the room, but the slick feel of the jade in her hand sends a soothing coolness through her blood, and she hesitates. Throwing a tantrum will not get her anywhere, especially if she offends a divine force by doing so.

'I am sorry,' she whispers, and sets the figure back down on the table. His expression, the exact opposite of her own, makes her conscious of the fact that her thoughts are her enemies; each one makes her as miserable as a lash from the cane. They bite directly into her soul and there is no escaping them and no turning away from them.

The door suddenly crashes open with all the menacing force of a powerful wing belonging to the serpent-like demon rushing in.

Isabella stumbles back in surprise as Lord Wulvedon's men stream into her bedroom. She cannot understand why he sent so many of them to deliver a single message or to fetch her to him. 'What…?' she gasps when the man who carried her to the library takes hold of one of her wrists, not at all gently, and stepping around her snatches the other one behind her back as well. But then she is distracted from wondering what he is doing as another man smiles at her, just before blinding her with a black cloth. 'What are you doing?' Her breathless cry is answered only by the sinister sensation of a rope slithering around her wrists in a complicated fashion before constricting, and eliciting a gasp of surprise from her at

126

how firmly her hands are bound without causing her any discomfort. Even the material covering half her face is pleasantly soft, and she does not really mind all she can see now is the fact that Lord Wulvedon ordered this done to her, which means he *was* thinking about her. But then her relief and happiness vanish when two strong hands grip the front of her dress, and rip it open.

'Mm, look at these sweet things…'

She is stunned when the simultaneous caress of two warm tongues makes her shamefully and intensely aware of her nipples. She tries to step back away from them, only to encounter the implacable wall of another man's body and the unmistakable fullness of a buried erection filling her hands. Shocked by the feel of it she steps forward again, and unwittingly presses her breasts even more effectively into two hot and eager mouths. The soft laughter of the men suckling her teats vibrates through her body and becomes confused with her own inner trembling… as though part of her is purring even while the rest of her stands stiff with denial as her breasts betray her heart…

'Mm, Isabella, I do believe you like being served by two men at once.'

'No,' she breathes. 'Stop!'

'Do not stop?'

'No,' she gasps, 'stop!'

'How does it feel to be a woman now, Isabella?'

'What do you mean?' She cannot believe Lord Wulvedon shared their intimate secret with all his men.

'All right, that is enough,' the voice in charge says curtly.

The air out in the corridor is startlingly cold against her stiff wet nipples as she thanks God they did not keep toying with her. The fingers digging into her arms tell her that her body is safe from any obstacles, but her heart feels poised on the edge of a precipice. Lord Wulvedon's growing affection and respect will either give her wings to fly or all her innocent hopes will crash to their death tonight.

With every blind step she takes, Lady Wulvedon's offer seems more and more appealing, hovering before her like a light in the darkness. Perhaps Bridget is right and she only believes she prefers men because she was raised that way. After all, what do men have to recommend them, exactly? Judging by the group around her, they use their physical strength to take advantage of others, they are not very communicative and they enjoy teasing helpless creatures. Lord Wulvedon has not expressed concern for her well-being, not as his sister has. It seems growing up without a mother has disadvantaged her and it might do her good to immerse herself in the feminine half of the world for a while. She has almost decided to accept Lady Wulvedon's offer when she remembers the way her three girls ripped her dress to shreds like drunken Maenads, and stumbles as much on her resolve as on the uneven floor.

Two of her escorts steady her between them. 'Careful there,' one of them says gently, and her heart melts for an instant because he sounds so very much like her father. She has no more say in what is going to happen to her than a child, and she gleans some comfort from the thought that once again she is going to learn something important. Lord Wulvedon is clearly intent on teaching her vital lessons, and even if some of them – *all* of them – hurt, it does not necessarily imply he means her harm and does not care for her, or so she desperately tells herself.

'We are almost there, princess.'

Tears spring into her eyes and dampen the cloth resting against them. 'There is no need to mock me, sir. It is bad enough you have bound me and blindfolded me and ruined one of the few dresses I own, and that you do not even have the courtesy to tell me where you are taking me, or why. So please, at least refrain from mocking me!'

For some reason the deep laughter her remark elicits from the men lifts her spirits, instead of rubbing salt into the wound as her mind tells her it should.

'What on earth makes you think I was insulting you, Isabella?'

'You know perfectly well I am just a governess and yet you call me *princess*.'

'You may be a governess, Isabella, but it was your natural nobility that inspired the endearment. Social status does not matter here, so do not worry about it.'

Her wounded feelings snap to attention. 'What *does* matter here?' She is thinking of her lovely reflection in the room's countless mirrors.

'I think you know, *princess*. Just be yourself.'

This command would have been easier to obey a few days ago when she had a much clearer understanding of who she was, or at least of who she *thought* she was.

They come to a stop, and she experiences the rush of displaced air as a door is opened. 'Watch your step,' the man to her right says as he pulls her forward gently. She cries out in alarm when her right foot suddenly fails to find the floor. 'It is a stairway, very steep and very long,' he informs her, and apparently it is also very narrow because the man on her left releases her. She wishes her hands were free to cling to her remaining escort's arm as her boot makes contact with a narrow ledge, then another one, and another one. Biting her lip, she falls into a careful rhythm with the solid warmth guiding her down, the cold void of space seeming to stretch forever on her other side as they descend straight down into the earth.

# Chapter Nine

Isabella sighs with relief when they finally reach the bottom, but then the man who accompanied her down lets go of her arm and she senses him move away from her.

'Where am I?' she asks anxiously, and what sounds suspiciously like another girl's helpless whimper coming from somewhere before her only makes the question more urgent.

'Where do you *wish* to be?'

The shock of Lord Wulvedon speaking directly behind her makes his voice seem to vibrate in the marrow of her bones. She immediately turns to face him, even though she cannot see him through the blindfold his men placed on her. 'I wish to be where I am, my lord.'

'But by your own admission, Isabella, you do not *know* where you are.'

'That is true, but you are here, so this is where I wish to be.'

'Are you sure?'

'Yes, my lord.'

'Then would you like to see for yourself where you are?'

'Oh yes, please.'

'Turn around.'

Her vision would have preferred to end its fast with his face so she could brace herself on his features and get some idea of what to expect from his expression, but she knows better than to protest. She obeys him at once, and it teases her to feel his fingers touching the blindfold as it slips away.

Warm tongues of torchlight lick her closed eyelids. She raises them cautiously, but the lighting is dim enough it does not take long for her eyes to adjust. Unfortunately, what she sees has an emotionally blinding effect on her.

She is standing in a large stone chamber she might mistake for a cave if it was not for the perfectly smooth walls and sharp, manmade corners. The sinister space is illuminated by torches, furnished with a variety of objects she does not even try to fit into her mind they all look so wicked, and decorated by naked girls chained to a wall.

'Welcome to the heart of the Castle, Isabella. It may be made of stone, but its soul is flesh and blood.'

'This is a torture chamber,' she whispers in horror. She has read about such places, but she could never quite bring herself to believe they truly existed.

'It is a chamber devoted to the sacraments of pain and pleasure, Isabella. Not one of these girls is here against her will. They have not been accused of witchcraft or of anything else. They are not being subjected to unendurable pain so they will confess their sins. In fact, they are encouraged to sin. But the important thing is they are all here because they *wish* to be here.'

She does not know why, it makes no sense at all, but she believes him. Perhaps because Juliet is one of the half dozen girls hanging like living tapestries against the cold stone – Juliet, who begged to be punished rather than sent away. Despite the unsteady light and all its masking shadows, Isabella recognizes her at once. She can now see the faces, and every other part, of her rivals. And as they all stare back at her, she suffers the impression a vast mirror has shattered and fragmented her own image so each shard catches and bends the light in a subtly he is approaching Juliet, and jealousy twists her insides, overwhelming her objective appreciation of his figure's fine lines. The heads of all the other girls turn to follow his progress with what strikes her as a disturbingly mindless unity, and at the same time she becomes aware that the shadows at the peripheries of her vision are alive with men. The chamber itself feels like a darkly sensual body in which Lord Wulvedon is the controlling mind, a body with a demonic heart of pulsing torchlight. She stepped out of the carriage and the Castle's monstrous jaws swallowed her whole. Now she is deep in its bowels, where all her hopes and dreams are being swiftly broken down and cynically digested by beastly appetites. And, most terrible of all, she is only one of its countless victims; there is nothing at all special about her suffering.

Her wrists strain uselessly at the ropes holding her hands impotently behind her back. Likewise, every clever, meaningful thought she has ever had in her life is as powerless as her fingers to pull her out of this terrifying abyss of sameness. She is not like all these other girls! She will *never* be like them! She is much more than flesh and bone at the mercy of blind animal desires. Yet she has no idea how she can prove this, at least not at the moment, not when her body is so busy reacting to what she is witnessing. When Lord Wulvedon reaches up and snaps open the manacle around Juliet's left wrist, she feels the other girl's relief, her excitement at the way he deliberately presses his body up against hers, and especially the effort she makes not to give in to the temptation to touch him. Her free hand hovers so longingly over his shoulder, Isabella bites her own lip in empathy.

She wonders how long all these girls have been chained down here like this, their bare feet planted against what is undoubtedly a cold floor, their arms bound loosely above their heads. She never realized how different bodies could be when stripped of the respectable sameness of clothing. Every bosom, large and small, every belly, every pair of thighs crowned by a spectrum of bushes, is as subtly different and as individually appealing as the face above them. At least these girls are not stretched painfully taut as Rose was, a mercy that strikes her as a small light in this dark nightmare. She feels as though she is dreaming as she watches Lord Wulvedon cup Juliet's breasts in his gloved hands and bend towards them. His back blocks her view, but the girl's sharp cry tells her he must have bitten rather than licked one of her nipples, as both of her own respond by tightening jealously. All the other captives writhe against the wall, obviously possessed by a similar sentiment, as he turns his attention to Juliet's other breast and elicits a second breathless scream from her. Whatever he is doing is too much for her because her hands fall on his head, either to hold it close or to push it away, there is no way to tell because he promptly straightens up and walks away from her.

'Come,' he commands, even as his eyes hold Isabella's.

Juliet follows him, obediently as a dog. Her long hair catches the torchlight as it falls forward when she lowers her head – miserably, humbly or both. She seems embarrassed by all the eyes on her, and surely she is at least nervous about what is going to happen to her. Isabella wonders if she knows what to expect or if this is the first time Lord Wulvedon will punish her, yet at the same time she is scarcely aware of Juliet as she tries desperately to grasp the thoughts behind Bernard's penetrating stare.

'As I mentioned, Isabella,' he lets the tips of her breasts kiss the black leather he wears like a second skin, 'there are different kinds and degrees of pain. Think of all the nerve-endings in your body,' he grips both her nipples between his thumb and index fingers, 'as different grapes that produce different kinds of wine, some sweet,' he pauses as she gasps and closes her eyes, 'and some, if taken to an even further extreme, incredibly potent, like cognac, otherwise known as the angel's share.'

She meets his eyes and braces herself on his stare, because for some reason it makes what he is doing to her breasts easier to bear. He is pinching her nipples and pulling on them and rubbing them relentlessly, transforming them into little flames radiating a hot torment through her chest. And somehow it does not surprise her to feel her pussy responding to the burning sensation by getting hopelessly wet as her wide eyes pour everything she is feeling into the crucible of his expression.

'Mm…' His mouth hardens even as he smiles. 'Matthew, kindly relieve Isabella of her skirt. Just leave enough of it to preserve her modesty.'

Her bosom heaves with mingled relief and indignation as he releases her nipples and turns back to Juliet, who is waiting a few feet behind him with her hands behind her back and her eyes lowered as though she finds her own bare feet fascinating. Her patient stance strikes Isabella as unnatural, and her utter submissiveness is almost supernatural, as if she is only the ghost of herself, hovering as close as she can to the dark energy emanating from him waiting for his will to animate her. He grabs her casually by the arm, his black glove a striking contrast to her creamy skin, and pulls her roughly over to a piece of 'furniture' Isabella does not have the chance to analyze before her attention is distracted by a man abruptly genuflecting before her. The blade in his gloved hand does not frighten her. In fact, she feels strangely calm as, holding the material up away from her thighs, he thrusts it into her brown skirt. Watching him cut through it, she feels hauntingly invulnerable, as if she is surviving the murder of her flesh. She parts her legs slightly, planting her boots firmly on the floor to brace herself as he moves around her, and she feels lighter and lighter as the heavy material falls away like the peel of a fruit. He straightens up, flinging the concealing curtain of her skirt away, and sheathes his knife. Then he slips one gloved hand up into the ragged tulip of cloth he left covering her hips and thrusts his other hand between her thighs, cradling her warm pink pussy in his cool black palm.

'Delicious,' he whispers in her ear.

The master of the Castle glances back at them even as he shoves Juliet face-forward over something vaguely resembling a portion of a fence.

Matthew withdraws his hand from between Isabella's legs with the comment, 'She could drown us all,' and steps back as Lord Wulvedon's intense stare pulls her towards him as effectively as a leash tied directly around the muscle of her heart, laboring beneath a rush of emotions.

Juliet is completely bent, only her toes touching the floor. The narrow wooden edge presses hard into her womb, but there is nothing she can do about it since Lord Wulvedon has bound her wrists to her thighs with a thin black rope, which cuts into her flesh and makes her hands look like aborted attempts at wings.

Isabella does not need to hear the other girl moaning to understand how excruciatingly uncomfortable her position is. There would seem to be no point to it except, as with the way Rose was hung up to be whipped, it enhances the lines of her body in a riveting way. Juliet is trying desperately but uselessly to put more weight on her toes to alleviate the pressure on her belly, her delicate bottom writhing invitingly in the pulsing firelight. When Bernard different way even as the intense need in her eyes is everywhere one and the same.

The chamber is large enough that her voice falls only on Lord Wulvedon's ears as she asks quietly, 'Are they all in love with you, Bernard?'

'They believe they are, Isabella.' His hands grasp her upper arms to prevent her from turning around to face him again, and even through her dress's long sleeves she can feel he is wearing gloves.

'You mean you do not believe them?' Her voice is breathless now from his touch.

His own voice drops to a whisper. 'What do *you* think?'

'I think they do not really know you and yet they believe they love you,' she replies, gazing remorselessly into her own soul through the eyes of all the lovely faces turned towards her. 'So naturally you do not believe them.'

'Naturally,' he agrees mildly. 'The truth is they are hopelessly in love with themselves, with their feelings and desires, with their dreams and their longings, which my wealth and position have the power to fulfill, or so they believe.'

'What you are saying is that they are in love with Lord Wulvedon and not with Bernard.'

His grip on her arms tightens for a second as if in painful confirmation of her observation before he releases her. 'Since you witnessed her transgression, Isabella,' he steps into her line of sight, 'I felt it only fitting that you witness her punishment as well.'

Her eyes follow the long line of his back and his legs walking away from her. The symmetry of his build almost hypnotizes her every time she sees it. His broad shoulders taper down to such narrow hips it makes her breathless to remember the length and width of the penis she has seen rise between them twice already. Then she realizes rests his hands on her cheeks, Juliet lets out a small cry, but all he does is give them a hard squeeze before stepping back to accept something one of his men hands him.

Isabella recognizes what up in the sunlit world would be an ordinary riding crop, but down here in a torch-lit dungeon the instrument possesses its own sinister personality.

'You know what a cane feels like, Isabella,' Lord Wulvedon turns towards her. 'My sister showed you no mercy. My guess is she wanted to break you, but she misjudged your strength.' Suddenly, he flicks the crop across the front of her thighs. He was holding her eyes and talking to her so pleasantly the gesture and the resulting pain come as a totally unexpected shock, hurting her feelings in every sense. 'You see? The riding crop is not as bad as the cane.'

She braces herself for another blow, but he turns away again and strikes the back of Juliet's thighs instead with a force that takes her own breath away just watching, and the quality of the girl's scream somehow tells Isabella she has never been beaten before; the disbelief, outrage and fear expressed in the cry make it clear Juliet is not merely reacting to the overwhelming physical agony.

'She is a virgin to punishment, Isabella, so I will be easy on her, much easier on her than my sister was on you.'

His sonorous voice and the way he moves enthrall her against her will. One second he looks perfectly relaxed, the next his arm lashes out like lightning. It is frightening yet also reassuring because of the control it expresses, and she needs to know he is in control of himself the more she feels she is not. Her mind insists she should be reacting to this scene with shock and despair, her body is going in a whole different direction, and like her wrists her heart and soul are hiding together somewhere behind everything.

She watches as Bernard brings the riding crop down hard across the nubile young buttocks offered up for him so invitingly. That Juliet is suffering terribly is the one thing in the world Isabella is sure of right now with her own thighs still stinging from just one casual blow. The girl's torment seems to deepen the shadows and brighten the torches as it concentrates everyone's awareness around it, like an utterly enthralling little fire they all huddle around attracted by the heat of her anguish as Lord Wulvedon remorselessly stokes it. She remembers what he said about being a priest, but obviously he does not settle for a symbolic vessel or a small piece of tasteless bread, which melts on the tongue as though it never was…

He tosses the riding crop away, grips Juliet's flaming bottom cheeks in his cool gloved hands, and bends over to slowly lick one of the hot trails he forged across her tender flesh. The tone of her cries changes as he separates her buttocks, and thrusts the tip of his tongue into her sphincter.

Isabella winces in disgust, as usual unable to believe what she is witnessing even as a shameful part of her relishes the sight.

Juliet moans with relief at being licked now instead of beaten, but her discomfort is obviously too great for her to enjoy anything done to her while she is forced to sustain her unnatural position. Isabella is wondering how she would feel about having Lord Wulvedon's tongue borrowing greedily into her own anus when he abruptly yields his place to Matthew, in such a way the helpless girl is probably not aware of the change; Juliet does not realize the hands holding her hips no longer belong to Bernard. Nor is it his erection plunging between her striped bottom cheeks and making her cry out again in shock and pain.

Isabella is appalled by the way the bound girl is being deceived, but there is also no denying the intense satisfaction she experiences knowing it is not Lord Wulvedon penetrating her. Mathew's stiff penis is slightly darker in color, and for some reason does not make the same impression on her, either visually or emotionally. What *is* making her breathless is Bernard's stare, which does not move from her face even as he sinks to his knees in front of Juliet. He lifts her head by the hair, and his cock finds her mouth the instant it rises out of his leggings. He effectively gags the blonde girl's cry with it, forcing her to swallow her protests as he carefully yet relentlessly slides his dick between her lips and fills her mouth. He weaves the fingers of both hands through her hair to hold her head up, and from the sounds she makes it is obvious she is not enjoying herself as one man packs his thick shaft into her tight little ass and another man caresses the swollen tip of his erection with her throat. Isabella knows Juliet must be wondering whom the cock ramming her from behind belongs to, and imagines she is at least grateful it is Lord Wulvedon plunging in and out of her face. Watching him, Isabella senses the lord of the Castle stimulating himself not only with the girl's lips and tongue, but also with her tortured expression and the pleading look in her eyes as she blinks up at him making a desperate effort not to gag.

Suddenly she is furious and disgusted, not only with the scene she is being forced to witness but with her own body's traitorous response to it. She is breathlessly torn between Matthew's pumping hips and Bernard's deceptively gentle rhythm, and there is no denying the excitement flashing in the increasingly deep and wet space between her thighs as she wonders what it would feel

139

like to be in such a vulnerable position herself. She is aware Lord Wulvedon's attention is divided between her rapt face and the one he is sliding his cock into, and the increasingly fierce cast of his features tells her what he sees pleases him. But then her attention is riveted on Matthew as his whole body stiffens, and he groans, a strangely lost look slackening his features as he wastes his seed in a girl's bottom.

When both her orifices are finally emptied, Juliet whimpers and sobs with relief, and Isabella is both terrified and thrilled to realize that, this time, Lord Wulvedon did not climax in her mouth. He lets the blonde head fall and smiles at Isabella as he rises, seemingly amused to see her eyes torn between his face and his rigid penis. It threatens her like a weapon she knows can hurt her. Yet it can also fulfill her in a powerful way when it is all hers… last night she felt it as a messenger he was sending into her body to tell her how much she means to him, how special she is to him, how much he wants her… but tonight the point he seems to be driving into her is that his cock does not belong to her any more than his heart does. Despair rises inside her and crashes in a blinding wave of anger as she remembers how trustingly she bled around him.

'If you are determined to destroy my belief in love and my faith in human nature, thereby murdering my soul, by forcing me to witness your cynical depravity, my *lord*,' she holds her head high as she defies him, 'you should be man enough to kill my body as well. Because without my soul my body is worthless, it is nothing but an empty shell of flesh and blood destined to sleep with the worms, and I have no desire to live without it, for I would not truly be living!'

'Isabella, you—'

'*What*, Bernard? Have you not the courage to take your actions as far as they must go in order to be truly complete? You torture the body but only murder the soul because there is no earthly court that can hold you accountable for this crime? I am not like all these other girls, I am not after your wealth and your power, nor am I content to merely exist as the mindless vessel of your pleasure. If there is any honor in you at all, you will kill my—'

A man's gloved hand falls over her mouth.

'Let go of her,' Lord Wulvedon commands.

Whichever one of his men sought to silence Isabella promptly releases her.

The wild words shaped by her tongue appear to have sharpened Bernard's desire even more than Juliet's whimpering helplessness, because his cock looks almost painfully hard. It clearly costs him some effort to close his leggings over it, after which he walks slowly towards her. 'Are you asking me to take your life, Isabella?'

His casual tone knocks the breath out of her and renders her speechless for a crucial instant, in which his smile sends a chill through her heart like a serpent slithering over it. 'Yes,' she gasps, and then manages to take a deep breath before repeating firmly, 'Yes, my lord, I wish you to set me free if this is all I can expect of life from now on.'

'Bernard,' one of his men says anxiously from somewhere in the shadows, 'this—'

'Be quiet,' Lord Wulvedon commands, and a profound silence falls over the chamber, in which the flickering shadows deepen menacingly. Even the quietly sinister music of chains ringing against stone fades away as all the girls stare at Isabella in open-mouthed disbelief and horror.

141

Coming to stand directly before her, Bernard stares down at her passionate countenance with nothing but a mildly curious expression on his own. 'Why do you believe I am trying to murder your soul, Isabella?'

'Stop trying to confuse me!' Tears fill her eyes and make it even more difficult for her to see him in the hellish light. 'You know perfectly well that is what you are trying to do, you and your sister both, even though she *pretends* to care for me. Honestly, I do not know which one of you is worse!' She does know she is working herself up into hysteria, but she welcomes the fervent release of tension that comes from expressing her deepest feelings, and which keeps all his attention riveted on her in a way she has yet to see it focused on any other girl… if she could only accomplish the same magic with his desire… 'I *hate* you, Bernard Wulvedon!'

He steps behind her and stuns her with how quickly he frees her hands. Her wrists had not ceased struggling against the rope, to no avail, and yet with just three swift tugs he whips it off her. Then he seems to pull the whole world out from under her as he lifts her up against his chest. Her arms slip around his neck and hold on to him; it does not occur to her to struggle. Even her thoughts rest quietly, infinitely heavy yet temporarily at peace in his embrace, the strength of which embodies the power of his will, which she finds mysteriously comforting despite how much his words and actions distress her. How she feels in his grasp makes no sense, but it does not matter. All she cares about is that her life is in his hands and she is making him take full responsibility for his actions.

Her unnatural calm only deepens when he lays her on her back across a cold stone surface, which immediately makes her conscious of how warm her skin is, how soft and vulnerable, and of just how easy it will be to expose her soul. There is barely anything left of her dress except the long sleeves and the back and a fragment of the skirt, and her hair flows wildly around her because she did not run a comb through it all day anymore than she was able to untangle her feelings. She is an absolute mess in every sense, and it distresses her to think she is going to see her father again looking like this. But it is too late to protest now. Lord Wulvedon has already strapped her wrists over her head. If she had realized there was a sacrificial altar waiting in the shadows perhaps she would not have been so hasty to offer him her life. Yet instead of frightening her she finds the very serious way he stares down at her profoundly reassuring. Her body is on a level with his hips, so he has to bend over to kiss the side of her left breast. Her heart takes off beneath the cool, firm pressure of his lips like the edge of a blade cutting through all her defenses.

He straightens up. 'Why are you offering me your life, Isabella?'

'I do not know…' Tears well up in her eyes again. 'My soul belongs to God, I know this, and yet…' Her voice drops to a whisper as if she is confessing a mortal sin. 'And yet I want it to be yours as well…'

A powerful emotion tugs on the corners of his mouth. 'You are confusing me with God, Isabella?'

'Yes, my lord.' She had not realized it, but it is true, this is exactly what she is doing, what she has been doing ever since she saw him silhouetted against the sunset. 'I cannot help it…' She cannot help it that since the moment she saw him she has been possessed by the sense he can make everything wrong with the world right. From the instant she heard his voice she felt he could help her because he understood her. And even now she still senses something special about him, a nobility having nothing to do with his title. Her faith in him is irrational and foolish and hopelessly naïve, yet it overpowers every other feeling inside her.

He leans over her again and smoothes the hair away from her forehead. 'Why do you have such faith in me, Isabella?' he asks gently.

'I do not know,' she repeats, frustrated she can offer him no better explanation, 'I simply do.'

'Why?'

His warm breath distracts her from the question as it seems to blow all her thoughts away and makes her tongue long to speak with him in a much more direct, wordless way. 'Please...' she begs softly.

'Please kiss you?' He brings his mouth teasingly close to hers. 'Or please kill you?'

She moans and tugs on the straps pinning her wrists down.

'Why do you have such faith in me, Isabella?' he asks again relentlessly.

She focuses on his features, on the fine lines of his face, which have captivated her from the moment she saw it, and suddenly the answer comes to her in a breathtakingly lucid rush of emotion. 'Because I can see your soul, Bernard,' she declares, and the way he straightens up abruptly makes it clear her answer surprised him. 'You try to hide it, but I can see it,' she goes on fervently. 'I thought it was the glow of the sun setting behind you, but it is your soul I saw the evening I arrived, and it is so intense and so beautiful... it must be why you always wear black, because it is like the shadow you cast... but when you are acting so cold, Bernard, it is not really you... not *really*.'

The way he stares down at her makes her wonder what

possessed her to believe in him. He looks so angry she is afraid he is about to comply with her passionate request and take her life. When he moves abruptly she cringes and quickly bends her knees up against her breasts to cover as much of herself as possible. Then she cries out when half the altar she is lying on seems to crumble beneath her, which makes her glad she pulled her legs up since there is nowhere to rest them now… except in his gloved hands as he grips her just below the knees and pushes her thighs open and steps between them. He bends over, and with a low guttural sound very much like a growl buries his face in her labia.

She gasps as her hands cling to the ropes around her wrists to brace herself. She can feel the shape of his features – the sharp bridge of his nose, his hard mouth and the rough trail of his goatee – pressing into the soft, moist warmth of her mortal clay, on which he is making an incredible impression. She feels as though he is casting his face in her pussy's mysterious heat so there is no way she will ever be able to forget it, not now she knows not only what his intense expression looks like, but what it *feels* like as well. He is eating her alive just as she watched him eat Rose, but much more furiously; he was not angry with the other girl as he is with her.

'Oh my lord!' she exclaims, staring blindly up into the darkness. 'Please… please stop!' She writhes against the rough stone while keeping a firm grip on the ropes over her head for fear she will plunge off the edge of the altar straight into his mouth, and there will be nothing left of her then. Yet her pleas only seem to make him more ravenous. He shakes his head against her like a mad dog, and shifts her thighs in his hands to pull her vulva even harder against his face. She dares to lift her head to look at him, but her mind cannot make sense of what she sees or of why the vision sends such a dark thrill through her blood. Her head falls back against the stone again and she feels as though he truly *is* killing her, not with a sword or a knife but with his teeth and the tender blade of his tongue as he thrusts it inside her. Breathless cries flow from between her lips, and vaguely she worries about drowning him she feels so impossibly wet and bottomless…

'Mm…' he moans. 'Mm… Mm…'

His deep voice vibrating through her womb sends her over some mysterious edge. 'Oh my lord,' she breathes, 'my lord!' as she suddenly finds her hips riding his tongue's swift strokes. She glimpses a stunning fulfillment looming on the horizon of her flesh she simply must reach now no matter what, and she goes from thinking he is killing her to feeling she will die if he stops. Then she realizes her cries are not the only ones rising above the hot crackling of the torches, and turning her head to one side, she opens her eyes.

The girls chained to the wall are at the mercy of large black wolves lapping at their pussies. The illusion lasts a split second in the flickering shadows; it is actually Lord Wulvedon's black-clad men crouched before the bound girls. Meanwhile, Juliet is still helplessly bent over and being forced to serve another man kneeling before her, his hips rocking selfishly back and forth in the face of her breathless torment.

Isabella can both hear and feel Lord Wulvedon's groans of satisfaction intensifying against her as a sensation like the sun rising directly between her thighs blinds her. 'Oh Bernard!' she cries. 'Bernard!' And his deep growl of triumph as her soul seems to pour straight out of her into his mouth is the most eloquent sound she has ever heard.

# Chapter Ten

Birds are just beginning to greet the new day, marking their territories with distinctly lovely little songs, unconcerned by the starkly naked branches of their homes. Shadows are soft and deep in these moments just before the sun banishes them all, the air beneath the trees a velvety gray blending with Lady Wulvedon's riding outfit and making the hair piled up beneath her matching hat shine like the eastern horizon.

Isabella takes another deep breath of the invigoratingly cold morning air, which she missed more than she realized. It is a pure delight to her lungs after the heavy atmosphere of her candle-filled room. Splendid as her accommodations at the Castle are, they cannot begin to compare with the humble magic of woodlands just before sunrise.

Lady Wulvedon sent Ludly to wake her and inform her she planned to go for an early morning ride, and her young tutor was to accompany her. Isabella, however, did not feel fit to accompany anyone anywhere except to bed, and sleep. The old man had a devil of a time rousing her, using his amazingly powerful voice to broadcast how displeased Bridget would be if she turned down this very generous invitation to join her. Eventually, the memory of the 'tree' on which she was hung as the cane sliced into her skin penetrated the sleepy fog of her brain, and she sat up. But it took her a few more minutes to pull her consciousness free from dreams of black wolves and fires burning in the night, and to focus on Ludly's ashen hair and wrinkled face. Once she did it made her think of a piece of paper someone had crumpled up and then tried to smooth out again. If there had been something important written on his expression once it had faded over the years or circumstances had smudged it out.

'Will you get up and dress now, miss?'

She blinked at him, rubbed both her eyes with her fists like a little girl, blinked at him again, and asked, 'Why are you here, Ludly?'

'To wake you, miss,' he answered patiently, 'and inform you that—'

'I mean, here at the Castle.'

It was his turn to blink a few times. 'Why do you want to know, miss?'

'Do you like it here?' she asked him earnestly, and woke up completely when he actually smiled.

'Oh yes, miss,' he replied, allowing his eyes to travel down her shift, something else he had never done before.

Not at all sure she really wanted to know the answer, Isabella nevertheless felt compelled to enquire, '*Why* do you like it here?'

'Because, miss,' he turned away and began lighting more candles, 'there are certain… benefits.'

*Like girls chained to the wall who cannot resist anyone's advances?* She promptly suppressed the thought by getting up.

Now Lady Wulvedon smiles at her from where she sits proudly astride a beautiful chestnut stallion wearing the length of her skirt as elegantly as a cape, and at the moment, Isabella sees no reason not to smile back at her. It does not matter she knows Bridget is wooing her, the exquisite burgundy riding outfit she had made for her poor little teacher part of the seduction. Infinite reflections of herself in a mirror, placed directly in front of another mirror exactly like it, told Isabella Bernard would approve

148

of her in this dress, and that is all that matters right now. Staring at her image in the glass, she looked from her face to the one behind it and to the one behind that, and on and on until she finally had to turn away from her unending image. She suffered a haunting vertigo trying to make out her last infinitely distant figure, which proved impossible in the end. The Isabella in the wine-colored dress and plumed hat showing off her dark hair and white skin truly did go on forever and ever. She discovered the two perfectly aligned mirrors this morning, and even as her horse trots over the frozen ground part of her is still there gazing into one room after the other, all of them exactly the same and yet somehow different. She suffered the haunting impression that in each reflection there were doors she could not see leading somewhere else, and that someone she did not know or has yet to meet or she knew before in another life might suddenly appear behind her...

'Isabella, dear, where are you?'

She jumps in the saddle and her nut-brown mare shakes her head in slight consternation at having her bit pulled for no good reason, for she was moving along at a perfectly pleasant pace.

'You are so far away this morning,' Bridget remarks indulgently, but then adds pointedly, 'again.'

'I was just thinking about reflections and reality, my lady.'

'Ah... you discovered the magic spot in your room where all the mirrors meet?'

'Yes.' She is wondering where Bernard is right now, and if he knows she is out with his sister. Probably not, as she imagines he is still asleep. Her grip tightens on the reins as her emotions clench around an image she tries to avoid just as she leads her patient mare around an obstacle in their path... Lord Wulvedon asleep, his long bare back pale as snow against black satin sheets twisted around his hips, his arms wrapped around... not Juliet or any of those others girls who had been chained to the wall... his arms are wrapped around a feather pillow, nothing more...

'My, my, Isabella, you certainly look determined about something all of a sudden. Are you perhaps thinking about my proposition?'

She is not obliged to answer right away as they both concentrate for a moment on guiding their mounts down a steep incline while admiring a breathtaking view of rolling hills framed by dense forests, and the sun rising over what appears to be a vineyard. 'I have not ceased thinking about your generous offer, my lady,' she replies once they reach level ground again.

'But you are still obsessed with my handsome, heartless brother?'

'I cannot believe he is heartless,' she declares stubbornly, hard-pressed to keep her tone light.

'Believe what you will, Isabella, but the truth always comes out in the end. You are wishing he could see you in your lovely new riding habit, are you not?'

'It is beautiful, thank you,' she answers evasively.

'Well, I am afraid you will not get your wish as my brother has gone away for a few days.'

Isabella is surprised her horse does not come to a dead stop, as her heart seems to do for a terrible instant. 'Where has he gone?' Her voice is listless because it does not really matter. The fact is he is gone, and suddenly the beauty of the morning means nothing; it may as well be a lifeless painting for all the power it has to move her now.

'He has gone,' by contrast Bridget's voice is languid with satisfaction, 'to see to our holdings. It cannot be all play and no work, you know. My brother enjoys almost as many responsibilities as he does pleasures. But what is it, dear? You cannot possibly miss a man you do not even know.'

Isabella has lost all interest in the conversation. Bernard is gone and she will not see him for days. Last night his face was buried between her thighs, his tongue was digging into her throbbing pussy, his warm, dry breath merging with her wet heat in an indescribably pleasurable way as his goatee roughly caressed her, his savage groans vibrating through her body and thrilling her beyond comprehension. Now he is gone, gone, gone…

'Isabella,' Bridget says sharply, successfully hooking her attention, 'you must come to your senses at once. You must cease mooning over an illusion, over a fairytale dream engrained into you from birth. Come now, you are a smart girl,' her tone softens and sweetens as she makes an effort to coat the bitter truth with the honey of flattery to make it easier to swallow, 'you are perfectly capable, if you really want to, Isabella, of looking your unconscious thoughts and desires in the face just as you looked at all those reflections of yourself this morning. You simply have to make an effort to find that magically objective place inside you. For you, my brother is both the villain and the prince of all the romantic stories you were raised on. He is an archetype a part of you cannot resist. But what you feel has nothing to do with him as a real live flesh and blood person. He is a man with a flawed personality, Isabella, not an ideal myth, and unless you snap out of it you will discover the hard way there is a big difference.'

'Why do you hate your brother so much, Bridget?'

She lets out an incredulous little laugh. 'I *love* my brother. I simply do not idealize him as you do because I know him as you do not. I have lived with him all my life.'

'Well, I think the truth lies somewhere in the middle, my lady.' She imbues as much finality into her conclusion as possible, because she really does not have the strength for this conversation today and she is eager to pursue her own thought as they ride.

Simply because Lord Wulvedon ate her alive last night does not mean he cares for her. At least he refrained from killing her as she so foolishly requested he do, even though every time she remembers what he did to her she is somewhat amazed her body survived the overwhelming experience, the climax of which literally felt very much like her soul bleeding straight out of her flesh into his mouth. It also thrills her to remember how hungry she made him. The more he devoured her, the more he seemed to want her, and this in turn leads her to recall her first evening in the Castle, when she attacked Lady Wulvedon in a similar fashion…

Blushing, she glances at Bernard's lovely sister and catches Bridget staring at her with the expression of someone attempting to solve a puzzle they find entertaining. However, her slight frown indicates she is beginning to suspect she is missing a vital piece, which frustrates her and makes her angry. The chill that travels down Isabella's spine then has nothing to do with the cold December morning as a vision of the 'tree' she was chained to momentarily obscures her view of all the living trees around her.

Bridget turns her horse around abruptly, causing Isabella's gentle mare to follow suit nervously. 'I am starving,' she announces. 'Let us head back for breakfast, shall we?'

The question is rhetorical; they are already galloping back towards the Castle. Even from a distance its scale is daunting. Isabella wonders if there are still girls chained to the wall down in a dungeon chamber not visible from the outside world. She prays they were released, because if they were not then Bridget is right and she is hopelessly wrong about Lord Wulvedon. He could not possibly be so cruel as to leave girls in chains all night, cold and naked and hungry. If she herself was carried all the way back to her room by one of his men, then surely those other girls were also released and allowed to sleep in warm, soft beds. Yet there is no way for her to know if this is the case or not, they might all still be down there suffering, with no one to hear their cries...

Her horse passes Lady Wulvedon's when she kicks her in the ribs trying to escape this highly disturbing thought, and Bridget takes this as a sign she wishes to race her back. Laughing, she forces her much faster stallion ahead of her tutor's again, and over the thunder of hooves Isabella suddenly hears Bernard's voice in her head saying 'None of these girls is here against her will', and at once she is completely reassured about the comfort and safety of her rivals as well as exhilarated to know it was *her* pussy he nearly drowned himself in. She reins into the courtyard only a few moments after Lady Wulvedon, who dismounts without the assistance of the grooms running out to meet them.

'I see your father taught you how to ride, Isabella.' She gives her stallion a fond parting caress on the neck with her gloved hand, and the way the powerful animal lowers his head in submissive pleasure at her touch sparks a sense of foreboding in Isabella. She was strangely, wonderfully elated this morning until she heard the news of Bernard's departure, and now a small voice inside her warns her this happiness is dangerous. She cannot forget the reality of her situation. She is only a naïve, penniless orphan in the hands of highly jaded nobles doing whatever they please with her and not even bothering to hide the fact.

As she accompanies Lady Wulvedon back into the Castle, walking just slightly behind her out of respect for their very different social positions, she wonders at how lighthearted she felt before she learned the master of the house was gone and would not return for a few days. As if her emotions are lamps, all the flames inside them seemed to go out and only his return will rekindle her energy and enthusiasm. There is nothing her rational mind can do about it, either. Knowing she should not feel this way, that she will more likely than not be hurt in the end, does not help her feel any differently. Not even when she was grieving for her dead father did she experience such intense ennui as a result of someone's absence. Bernard has gone away and taken her soul with him...

Perhaps what she is suffering now is God's displeasure, Isabella thinks worriedly. It would explain why all the beauty went out of the world when she heard Lord Wulvedon was gone, because surely the Creator cannot be expected to share custody of her soul with a mere mortal. Perhaps she has committed a grave sin by offering herself to a man so completely, and cut herself off from divine grace by giving herself, body and soul, to an earthly power in the form of a handsome nobleman. The concept would be disturbing if she could believe it, which she cannot. In the literature of most cultures love is a sacred mystery, and whatever Lord Wulvedon's intentions, she knows loving him may be foolish but cannot possibly be a sin.

A sumptuous breakfast has been delivered to Bridget's room and laid out on low oriental style tables. The lady of the manor flings her hat and gloves away carelessly, confident someone will pick them up after her later, and sinks gracefully to her knees in front of a painstakingly polished silver tea service.

Isabella remains standing, not sure where she is supposed to sit, the plume of her hat making her want to sneeze as she sets it respectfully down on a small table.

Bridget smiles up at her. 'No need to be so formal, Isabella, come and eat. Girls, breakfast is served!' She sighs. 'They are the laziest little pussies I have ever owned.'

Isabella chooses to sink, a little stiffly, to her knees beside the lady of the house.

Rose is the first to appear, her fiery hair concealing most of a thin shift, and her face still blank with sleep she looks at least five years younger than she really is. Isabella cannot believe this is the same girl who offered herself up to be whipped with such graceful willingness, yet it is undoubtedly her, for beneath the misty material of Rose's nightgown she can make out the whip's faint red signatures. And glimpsing these marks now through the innocent white fabric makes them seem even more sinister to Isabella than they did when she saw them being forged across the girl's tender skin. In a similar fashion, last night has left evidence of its reality on *her* she cannot ignore. Her pussy still aches from the imprint of Lord Wulvedon's features, and her nipples have not forgotten what it felt like when he was torturing them; she has been aware of them all morning pressing up against her bodice, still smoldering from so much violent attention. Bridget's choice of words when describing her relationship to her girls is also disquieting. *Owned…* only a slave can be owned.

Rose hesitates when she realizes one of the choice spots beside Lady Wulvedon is taken, and Isabella detects a series of emotions flashing in the other girl's eyes which does nothing to improve her appetite. But apparently

Rose's hunger is greater than anything else she might be feeling, because after a bristling second she smiles, and seats herself directly in front of her mistress. She refrains from reaching for any food, however, clearly needing permission to do so first. Isabella seriously doubts she is waiting for Bridget to say grace.

Elaine and the nameless girl enter the room hand-in-hand, their uncombed hair and sleepy eyes giving them the appearance of bravely leading each other out of the wonderfully uncomplicated realm of dreams. In a way they are lovelier in this unkempt and vulnerable state than when their faces are painted and opulent gowns distract from the rosy softness of their skin, hiding their smoky nipples and the glowing shadows of their pubic hair, distinctly visible through their nearly transparent shifts. They do not react to the young teacher's presence at all as they seat themselves to the left of Rose.

How Lady Wulvedon's girls feel about her makes no difference whatsoever to Isabella. The most vital part of her being is still lying across a stone altar with Bernard's head buried between her legs. She wishes she could have stayed with him afterwards, or that he had at least said something to her, but he merely held her eyes for a long, sober moment before turning away. She was so mysteriously drained by how energetically he feasted on her she was barely aware of one of his men freeing her hands. Then he scooped her effortlessly up in his arms and carried her all the way back to her room. She suffered a few seconds of real fear when he set her down, yanked off what remained of her dress, and lifting her naked body again carried her over to the bed. But he simply laid her across it and left…

'You are being rude, girls,' Lady Wulvedon's voice breaks through Isabella's reverie. 'Bid good morning to Isabella, who will, I hope, soon be your loving sister.'

'Good morning, Isabella,' all three girls speak up in pretty harmony.

Her eyes linger on Rose, who has also had the honor of feeling Lord Wulvedon's tongue in her pussy. For all she knows, he has tasted every one of them. 'Good morning, Rose,' she says. 'Good morning, Elaine, and good morning... I am sorry, I still do not know your name.'

'Melody,' the third girl replies in a quiet, husky voice.

'Good morning, Melody.'

Lady Wulvedon picks up the teapot, fills Isabella's cup after hers, and then sets it back down. Her girls will obviously have to help themselves. 'Sugar, Isabella?'

'Yes, two lumps, please. Thank you.'

'Cream?'

'Yes, thank you.' It makes her nervous the lady of the house is waiting on her, especially since there is no way she can accept her proposition, not now and not ever. Once more Lord Wulvedon's voice rings in her head, drowning out the delicate chiming of porcelain cups against saucers, 'She prefers men'...

Silver platters have been artfully arranged with a variety of sliced fresh fruits, a true luxury in the middle of December, and there are small silver goblets of what appears to be curdled milk. Isabella looks skeptically down at the one Bridget slides her way.

'It is yogurt, Isabella.' She smiles indulgently at her expression.

'Yogurt?'

'Milk that has been allowed to go bad for days and days until it is ripe with bacteria,' Rose explains with morbid eagerness.

Isabella thinks it is a good thing she is not very hungry, because nothing on the table appeals to her much; she has always preferred vegetables to fruit. And where, she wonders, is the freshly baked bread, salted butter, fried eggs, crisp bacon and warm milk that, in her opinion, constitute a real breakfast? She contents herself with sipping her tea, ignoring the yogurt whilst dreaming of a soft-boiled egg accompanied by a steaming hot slice of lavishly buttered bread.

'Isabella, you must eat,' Lady Wulvedon commands nicely.

'I do not much care for fruit,' she admits, 'or *yogurt*, thank you.'

Elaine and Melody glance at each other as Rose casts her an oddly sympathetic glance. Rose, who Isabella feels a resentful affinity towards remembering Bernard smiling at her as he raised his face from between the girl's whip-burned thighs...

'What? You do not care for fruit?' Bridget is incredulous. 'I never heard anything so absurd. Fruit is the most delicious and healthful food on earth.'

'Perhaps she would prefer a nice big cucumber,' Melody suggests, and Elaine quickly pops a fig into her mouth to suppress a giggle.

'Be quiet and eat,' Bridget snaps, and everyone obeys at once, including Isabella, who picks up a silver spoon and dips reluctantly into her yogurt. It tastes as terrible as it looks. She wonders if it is only her imagination or if Rose truly keeps looking her way as if she wants to tell her something, which in turn leads her to wonder how the other girl ended up in the Castle. Was she also somehow forced into 'service'? Is she happy here with Lady Wulvedon? Yet why then did she react so passionately when Lord Wulvedon, a man, was eating her?

She is so lost in thought she does not notice right away that Melody and Elaine have begun playing with each other.

The blonde girl is caressing the other girl's straight brown hair away from her neck so she can nibble on it as though it is just another part of breakfast, except this particular dish is alive and can respond to the act of being consumed. She does so by turning towards her gentle attacker and gripping one of her nipples through her shift. She rubs it between her fingertips in a way Isabella's own breasts immediately respond to as Elaine moans, and leaning back on her arms offers her other nipple up to the same treatment. Only it is Rose who gets to it first, capturing it between her teeth through the thin fabric covering it and flicking the rosy tip of her tongue over the firm little stamen. Elaine throws her head back with a gasp and, watching her, Isabella feels an exquisite warmth kindle between her legs. Yet watching is all she desires to do; she does not feel the urge to caress Elaine herself. It is more as if her body enjoys identifying with what is being done to the other girl, so when Melody shoves Elaine onto her back, her own breath catches in response. She can see the blonde girl's pointed breasts rising beyond the platter of fruit framed by the pyramids of her legs, which bend and spread open after her shift is impatiently pulled up over her head by four hands. She is as naked now as the peeled fruit, but in Isabella's opinion she looks much more deliciously edible.

'Would you like to observe more closely, Isabella?' Lady Wulvedon asks her.

'Yes,' she says, mainly because she knows it is the proper response.

'Then by all means do so, they will not mind. Sit behind her, that will give you a nice view.'

Isabella rises, moves around the table, and kneels behind Elaine, who promptly lifts her head onto her lap and uses it as a pillow to prop herself up while she watches her friends playing with her. The real breakfast is completely forgotten as Melody and Rose each take one of Elaine's breasts in both hands and squeeze while sucking on her hard nipples, making Isabella think of seeds being forced out of a fruit's soft pure pulp. Elaine's arms reach blindly up behind her as she moans, and without any idea she intended to do so, Isabella captures her wrists so her searching hands fall over her own breasts. Elaine gasps and tries to get a good grip on them, but the firm bodice frustrate her efforts. Fortunately it closes down the front and Isabella hastily undoes enough of the little hooks to pull open the dark-red fabric. The instant she exposes her firm bosom, Elaine fills her hands with it eagerly, sighing and writhing in mingled pain and pleasure as Rose and Melody continue tormenting her own increasingly rosy orbs. Isabella experiences the physical sensation of her touch, but nothing more. It is decidedly pleasurable, but in a superficial way that does not take root inside her. Being touched herself enhances her arousing view of the other girl's nipples being licked and bitten and cruelly tweaked between long fingernails, yet part of her is already growing bored…

'Enough,' Lady Wulvedon says impatiently.

Elaine's whole body stiffens in protest at being taken to this point and then abandoned, but she obediently lets go of Isabella just as Melody and Rose reluctantly release her.

'Isabella, you have the most expressive face I have ever seen,' Bridget comments as she rises and moves around the table towards her. 'Your thoughts are written on it almost as clearly as words on a page, and what I see is that you are merely titillated by this little scene, which displays a remarkable amount of self-control for a virgin.' She grabs a handful of Isabella's hair and yanks her painfully to her feet by it.

'Let go of me!'

Lady Wulvedon's response to her angry cry is to pull on her roots. A burning anguish radiates through her skull and she has no choice but to stumble along behind her gracious hostess. *Oh God, not the tree* she thinks *please, God, not the tree! And not the cane!* but pride keeps her from actually giving voice to this plea, as does the knowledge that it would be futile to do so. Bernard is not here to protect her, not in his sister's quarters, not in the Castle at all. He is gone and she is completely at Bridget's mercy.

'Strap her in,' Lady Wulvedon commands.

The intense relief Isabella feels when her hair is finally released blurs her vision as her eyes fill with tears, therefore she does not get a clear view of the chair into which Melody shoves her. The seat is as hard as a saddle, and so precariously narrow she is afraid of slipping off it when hands grasp both her ankles and abruptly raise and spread her legs, forcing her to lean back against the chair's equally hard and narrow back.

She blinks the salty indignation out of her eyes and watches with a strange sense of calm as her feet are thrust into stirrups crowning two widely spaced spear-like poles rising out of the floor. Her ankles are bound firmly with leather straps, and then Rose and Elaine each grab one of her hands and stretch her arms straight up over her head, where her wrists suffer the same fate. Her long red skirt is then bunched up around her waist so her pussy is fully exposed, along with her breasts. She does not need to test the straps to know she is utterly helpless, and Bernard has no idea what is being done to her. Yet if he knew, would he even care? Fortunately, she does not have time to ponder the question. She is too busy anxiously studying

161

the object Lady Wulvedon is holding.

'Isabella, my dear,' she comes and stands between her young teacher's legs, 'it is time you lost the virginity you are so proud of. It is nothing but a worthless piece of skin valuable only to men because it makes them feel powerful and important to possess what no one else has, to conquer it like generals invading unclaimed territory.'

'My lady, please do not do this…'

'I am doing you a favor, my dear. A woman has a foolish and usually disastrous tendency to fall in love with the man who deflowers her. I am sparing you that danger, while at the same time proving how ridiculous it is, by initiating you into womanhood with an ivory penis. You are not about to fall in love with part of an elephant's tusk, are you?'

'Too late, my lady,' Isabella retorts coolly. 'I am already in love with your brother.'

Bridget sighs and holds the stone phallus up to admire its inhuman dimensions. 'You disappoint me, Isabella. I was sure you were intelligent enough to…' Her green eyes widen as though she suddenly sees something she cannot believe. 'No,' she says quietly, 'it cannot be.' She is talking to herself now, but her self does not appear to be convinced because she says again, 'He would never…' The cruel looking dildo falls to her side, forgotten. 'He has never disrespected me by taking what was mine behind my back, *never*.' She stares fixedly into her young tutor's eyes for a long moment. Then suddenly her beautiful face hardens and she roughly thrusts the ivory cock between Isabella's labial lips, sinking the cold and ancient erection into her tight young pussy until all that is left exposed is the thick end she grips in her clenched fist.

Isabella does not scream during the brutally swift penetration, which is too excruciatingly painful for her to waste any strength protesting it; she has to focus all her energy on enduring the invasion. And it hurts even more when Bridget wrenches the lifeless cock back out, cleaving her open around its monstrously thick and unyielding length. Isabella has never heard anyone howl in rage before, and the sound is made even more terrible when it blends with her own wail of anguish as the stone phallus forces her throbbing pussy open around it again. She looks breathlessly down at the animal tusk; grateful she was at least a little wet from watching the girls playing with each other as her body miraculously absorbs the dildo's terrifying dimensions.

'You little slut,' Bridget coos.

'Oh God, you are hurting me!'

'Am I?' Lady Wulvedon twists the cold shaft from side to side as if trying to screw it even deeper into Isabella's cleft. 'Does it hurt as much as when you bled around my brother's hard cock?'

'It hurts more! Oh God, it cannot go any deeper, please…'

'What makes you think God cares about a little whore like you, if He exists at all?'

Isabella sucks desperate, shallow breaths in through her mouth watching as her body is violated, because watching enables her to hold on to the illusion she has some control over what is happening to her. But then Elaine and Melody pounce on her breasts like two starving cats and she cannot help but close her eyes and grit her teeth as they suck viciously on her sensitive nipples. Then it is really just too much when Rose starts kissing her. Her cool soft tongue tastes innocently of fresh fruit, and its sweet 'come out and play' attitude is an insult in the face of the violence she is enduring between her thighs.

'This is what you like, is it not, Isabella,' Lady Wulvedon

asks harshly, 'a big, hard, selfish dick using you? If you truly prefer men, you must love this.'

'No, it is cold and lifeless and awful! Please…' her voice catches on a sob. 'Please, stop!'

'I am not going to stop until you come, you little slut, so I suggest you get to it. Just think about my brother. Close your eyes and imagine this is his greedy hard-on lodging itself deep in your precious little jewel box.'

She cannot beg for mercy because Rose gently gags her with her tongue again, leaving her no choice but to take her tormentor's advice. She imagines it is Bernard stabbing her with his erection as he bites her nipples, igniting a unifying trail of pain between her breasts and her pussy she follows deeper and deeper into her imagination, her heart beating Bernard, Bernard, Bernard…

'*Yes*,' Lady Wulvedon hisses, and bends over to flick the tip of her tongue angrily over Isabella's clitoris.

She climaxes sobbing into Rose's mouth, because the beautiful sensation is painfully empty without Bernard there to mysteriously catch her soul.

Bridget straightens up. 'I hope you enjoyed that, my dear, because it is the last taste of pleasure you will know for a very long time. Strip her and hang her.'

'No…' she protests weakly as Rose frees her wrists and Elaine and Melody perform the same favor for her ankles. 'No, let go of me…'

'Be quiet,' Rose whispers in her ear. 'There is nothing you can do about it, so just try and enjoy it. You *can*, you know.'

'You have lied to me, Isabella,' Lady Wulvedon accuses her, 'and seduced my own brother into betraying the understanding between us, something he has never done before. I trusted you, I trusted him, and the both of you betrayed me. I can forgive him, for he is after all only a man and, more importantly, my beloved brother, but *you* I cannot forgive, not until you have been properly punished. You must pay for your effrontery and your deceptiveness, and you must pay dearly.'

Elaine and Melody let her legs fall, pull her roughly up out of the chair and drag her over to the 'tree'.

She began the day listening to the sweet chirping of birds, now it is the sinister clinking of chains that fills her ears. *Bernard!* She thinks in terror and despair. *Oh, Bernard!*

# Chapter Eleven

Isabella has no idea how long she has been hanging from the 'tree'. The position she finds herself in is stretching time out as cruelly as it does her body; minutes feel like hours and hours might as well be days. She is disturbingly aware of her skeleton, of the bones her skin-clad muscles cling to so tenaciously in order to secure what she knows as life and awareness. It seems to her if she survives this ordeal she will be taller than she was before she arrived at the Castle. Her arms are raised straight up over her head, crossed and bound at the wrists, and she has to relax and stretch every joint and vertebrae she possesses to plant her toes on the cool stone floor in an effort to alleviate some of the burning in her shoulders. It also keeps her hands from falling asleep, which is what happens when she is forced to rest for a while and let all her weight hang from the rope. In those terrible moments, she feels like a freshly slain deer skinned of her clothes and hung in this perverse larder waiting to be tenderized by a cane or a whip or a riding crop. Then there is the cold, heavy chain around her waist pressing her against the pole and making it even more difficult for her to extend her body and put at least a fraction of her weight on the floor. Yet the most terrible thing of all, which fills her soul with a despair equivalent to the burning in her muscles, is that no one is present to witness her suffering and at least offer her the hope of ending it once they have finished taking pleasure from it. She appears to be completely alone in Lady Wulvedon's sumptuous chamber.

She continues discovering new and sinister details in the tapestry of the black knight on horseback. It looks very much like a complex rendering of a Tarot card, complete with the naked bodies of a man and woman falling hand-in-hand to their deaths almost as if they deliberately jumped out of the burning tower together. Her body increasingly identifies with the tower's slender flaming length, and the more time that passes without relief, the more her discomfort deepens to the point where she knows, where she is sure, she cannot endure it another second. Yet she does endure it, and the longer she succeeds in withstanding it, the more strangely detached she feels from herself and the more she identifies with the girl in the tapestry. The man, of course, is Lord Wulvedon, to whom her heart is holding onto desperately. And yet for what? According to Bridget, once she learns what he is truly like all her hopes and illusions will shatter like bones crashing to the ground from an idealistic height.

At first she concentrates helplessly on her plight, unconsciously stoking her suffering by focusing on it, but she soon realizes the only possible escape is to let her mind wander…

She tries to picture where Bernard is… she imagines him riding through his vineyards wearing a white shirt beneath a long-sleeved black vest laced loosely closed in front… but it would be cold this time of year, which means he is probably wearing a black cape and black gloves… she wonders if Lady Wulvedon will use the cane on her again or if she simply means to leave her here like this indefinitely, or at least until her brother returns…

Isabella is not sure whether she should be relieved or not when she thinks she hears someone enter the room. She holds her breath waiting to see who it is, allowing herself a wonderful daydream of Ludly sent to release

167

her and escort her back to her lavender bed…

It is Lady Wulvedon wearing a black and violet gown and holding a riding crop in one of her gloved hands. Half her hair is pinned up, the rest cascades down her back, soft and straight as a sunlit waterfall. Not even the shadow of a smile touches her mouth, which looks even thinner than usual beneath a blackberry lip color. 'I am going to give you a little taste of three different forms of punishment, Isabella,' she says coldly. 'A riding crop.' She holds it up. 'A whip.' She touches what Isabella mistook for a unique looking belt around her waist, one tapering end trailing halfway down her skirt. 'And just to remind you what it feels like,' she stretches her arm out and Melody steps into view in order to hand her mistress something, 'a cane. You will then choose which one you would prefer for the first course of your punishment, which will be the second and which the third, because you will endure them all, my dear. Your discipline will last three days, and you will be granted only a few moments' reprieve during that time so you may perform certain necessary bodily functions, but that is all. You will be given bread and water, once in the morning and once at night and, if you can manage to do so, you will sleep whilst hanging from the tree, where you will remain until your penance for lying to me, and for seducing my brother into betraying me, is complete. Do you understand, Isabella?'

'And after three days you will let me go, mistress?'

'I have not decided… perhaps not. You will stay as you are until I am certain you have seen the error of your ways and have truly repented your actions.'

'But you cannot—'

'I will allow you to guess what I am using on you.' Lady Wulvedon steps behind her, and Isabella gets her first excruciating clue across the small of her back. 'Which one was that?' Bridget demands.

She is too busy trying to catch her breath from the shocking pain to respond.

'Answer me!' Lady Wulvedon subjects her to another agonizing clue. 'I will not stop until you get it right.'

'A riding crop!' she cries. 'It is a riding crop!'

'Very good.' Bernard's sister strikes her again, this time across the highly sensitive backs of her thighs. 'Remember what it feels like,' she advises, and a moment later forces her to endure another blow, only this one hurts far more where it licks across her upper back.

'The cane!' she gasps in stunned recognition of the pain's distinctly cruel signature.

'Correct.'

She is rewarded with another searing caress, only this one slices into her bottom, which is still tender from her first taste of this merciless weapon, and she cannot help but scream as a new burning welt intersects with an old one to create a dimension of agony she could never have imagined. 'Why are you doing this?' she sobs. 'Why are you so cruel?'

'Oh Isabella, you are so delightfully naïve.' Lady Wulvedon punishes her for her innocence by once more bringing the cane down hard across her buttocks. 'I am doing this because I enjoy it, and because we all need guidance and discipline in our lives and you are in a crucial point in yours, my dear. But I am tired of explaining myself to you. You do not listen. What I am giving you now is a lesson on how to truly listen, not just with your ears and your head, but with every fiber of your being. Perhaps it will make you a little wiser, but whether it does so or not, you will certainly be more respectful, and you will certainly think twice before ever lying to me again.'

Isabella screams and screams as the cane cuts into the highly sensitive skin just beneath her straining shoulder blades.

'Well, which one is it to be first, the cane, the riding crop or,' Lady Wulvedon pauses to subject her to yet a slightly different form of agony, 'the whip?'

'The whip!' she gasps. 'Please, the whip!' Perhaps someone will save her before she has to endure the cane. She can only hope against hope and pray there is a God and that He will take pity on her. Yet what if Bridget is right and she has forfeited His mercy by so wantonly offering herself, body and soul, to a selfish and sinful man? What if she has damned herself and this is her first taste of hell?

The crisp, confident snap of the whip reinforces this terrible reasoning over and over again as it proceeds to mark nearly every inch of her body, beginning with her upper back and ending with the cripplingly tender area just above her knees. Lady Wulvedon and the whip are one purely terrible and determined force there is no fighting and no escaping, a fact she finally accepts after the tenth lash, when she is sure she cannot possibly survive another one. Yet she knows she will, which leaves her no choice but to take Rose's whispered advice and deliberately surrender herself to the torment... Instead of tensing in preparation for the next cracking blow and dreading it, she completely relaxes her body and accepts the leather strip's burning caress as if she has been rendered languid not by fear but by how intensely she desires it. And each time she succeeds in doing this, the more the agony of each hot lick begins to feel like an unbelievable, unbearable, indescribable pleasure...

'Isabella,' someone whispers in her ear. 'Isabella?'

She cannot quite manage to respond.

'Here, drink this,' the voice insists gently but firmly.

What she recognizes as the edge of a cup touches her lips, and because she does not have the strength to resist, a cool liquid flows onto her tongue and from there travels down her throat, which fortunately swallows reflexively without her having to make an effort.

'Good. Now eat this, quickly, it is some cheese I saved for you. You must eat it all. You are weak as a kitten from days and days of nothing but bread and water. You really made her angry, you know. I have never seen her be this cruel.'

Isabella is close to passing out again, this time from how delicious the sharp, firm substance in her mouth tastes. Her tongue is in ecstasy, and when she swallows the fresh cheddar lands in her stomach like an ounce of gold, buying her a few moments' reprieve from its clawing emptiness. But the ache of hunger is only one of endless notes in the symphony of torment being played with her bones and her muscles and her flesh, which feels as taut as the skin of a drum. The only good thing about her condition is all the vivid dreams and hallucinations she keeps having. At times she must be asleep, which makes them dreams, but at others she is relatively certain she is awake. She saw a painting of the *Taj Mahal* once in a book, and she keeps returning there now… she actually seems to be standing beneath the bright blue sky gazing up at the exquisitely carved spires and dome of the beautiful mausoleum, wondering if Lord Wulvedon will be romantic and passionate enough to have *her* bones made into flutes once his sister is done with her, and wondering what sort of music they will make – probably low, sad minor notes…

'Isabella, listen to me, you cannot continue to defy her. She will not stop torturing you until she thinks she has broken you. Do you understand me?'

She opens her eyes and holds onto Rose's anxious expression as she concentrates all her strength in her voice. 'Tell Bernard…'

'He will not care. And even if he does care, he will do nothing. She is his sister. They are loyal to each other.'

'Tell him, Rose.'

'Why do you believe you are so special, Isabella?'

'Because,' her eyes close again, 'my father always told me I was.'


Isabella opens her eyes, and holds her breath, awestruck by the intense clarity of this new hallucination. It is so exquisitely detailed she is filled with appreciation for the power of her imagination, which is even greater than all the vivid dreams she enjoys every night led her to suspect it was. Yet until now she was never able to harness its boundless energy with her conscious mind. She is familiar with the theory great pain and physical hardship can lead to altered, and often enlightened, states of being, and it thrills her to realize the books were right.

One of the many exquisite details of this particular hallucination is she seems to be lying down. A small, worried voice in her mind tells her she is still hanging from the 'tree', but she finds it easy to ignore this voice considering all the overwhelming sensual evidence to the contrary. Not only is she in a wonderfully recumbent position, her body is hidden beneath deliciously clean white sheets, her tortured bottom soothed by the infinitely soft feather mattress beneath it. The bed is not the lavender fairy bower of her candle filled chamber; it takes up only a modest corner of a small, rustically furnished room and affords her an excellent view out of a window located beside a rough wooden door. The dark-green curtains are pulled back so she can see outside, the snow-covered world a cozy extension of her comfortable white nest.

She cannot remember ever having been in a room like this before, but then she often dreams with people and places she has never seen. Her imagination has come up with a restful place to escape to furnished very much like the little townhouse in which she grew up – with unpolished wooden furniture and thick dark drapes to keep out the cold in winter and the hot sunlight in summer. Nevertheless, the details amaze her. She can see every crack in the weathered old nightstand beside her, every rough little bump in the whitewashed ceiling above her, and the view through the window is a breathtakingly crisp painting of snow-covered trees rising a few yards behind a stone well. She would appear to be recovering from her severe punishment in a peasant's humble one room cottage, which is permeated by the most divine smell…

Isabella turns her head on the pillows she is propped up against, and spots a black kettle hanging in a fireplace simmering a heavenly brew of meat and vegetables and herbs, that elicits a painfully passionate response from her stomach. If this is a hallucination, then she is perfectly happy to lose her mind.

The door leading out into the yard opens.

She clutches the sheets up against her chin, determined to hold on to them, and to the bed, and to everything else in this comforting fantasy.

An elderly woman enters the room, and to Isabella she is positively beautiful simply because she is not Lady Wulvedon.

'Ah, so you have finally come around.' She smiles at her young guest over the small woodpile cradled in her arms. 'Just in time for supper.'

Isabella regards the woman with a wide-eyed fascination she seems to find amusing, because she chuckles to herself as she turns away and places the firewood next to the hearth, bending and kneeling with impressive flexibility considering all the years imprinted in her face. She then dips a copper spoon into the simmering cauldron and stirs it for a long moment, which Isabella finds at once soothing and exciting she is so hungry. But apparently the stew is not yet ready, for she hangs the spoon back up on a nail thrust into the gray flagstones. She then bends over again and pulls something out of a stone shelf built into a corner of the fireplace – a loaf of bread, crisp and brown and an exquisite torture to Isabella's nose as she inhales the smell of freshly baked flour mixed with herbs and… cheese. *Cheese* bread! 'Where am I?' she gasps. 'And may I stay, please, at least for a little while?' Because if this is a dream, she knows what will happen. She will wake up just before the hot and flavorful stew touches her tongue, or just before she slips a piece of that deliciously fragrant bread into her mouth.

The old woman straightens up and turns back towards her, wiping her hands on the coarse brown apron she is wearing over a gray dress. 'Do not worry, dear, you are not going anywhere for a while.'

Isabella cannot understand why she looks so grim, for it is the best of news. 'Is this really happening?' she dares to ask.

'I am afraid so.'

'But… but I was in Lady Wulvedon's quarters, and I was—'

'Try not to think about that now, dear. Go back to sleep now.' She approaches the bed. 'I will wake you again when supper is ready.'

'Oh no, I cannot go back to sleep, because then I will end up back there. I have to stay awake!'

'No, dear, this is not a dream.' She rests a cool hand on Isabella's forehead. 'You see, I am real and you are safe,' she turns away again abruptly, 'for now.' She seats herself in a wooden rocking chair and smiles encouragingly at the young woman lying in bed as she takes up her knitting. 'Now go back to sleep and I promise I will wake you when supper is ready. My name is Carol and I am quite real, I assure you.'

'Carol… how did I get here? The last thing I remember I was—'

'Shush!' She claps her copper knitting needles together peremptorily. 'Do not think about that now. Lord knows you will never be able to forget it, but now is not the time to dwell on it, not when you need all your strength to heal your body. You can worry about the much deeper emotional wounds later – right now you need to rest.'

Isabella finds the woman's blend of realism and tenderness quite believable and, therefore, reassuring. 'Yes, madam.'

'My name is Carol,' her needles snap together again as she concentrates on her work, 'and I am not giving you an order. You can sleep if you like or you can stay awake. It is entirely up to you.'

Now Isabella is sure she is no longer in the Castle and her eyes close peacefully.

The rope grinds against the metal wheel turning it as she pulls, gritting her teeth, not from the weight of the bucket hanging from it, but because she is making an effort not to remember what it felt like when her body was similarly suspended. Of course, she thinks about it all the time, perhaps because she cannot remember the ordeal clearly

175

at all, and this bothers her. She cannot forget, however, that she achieved the impossible. Like the alchemists her father loved to read about, she transformed the base metal of pain into the magical gold of pleasure, and with each night she passes in the cottage, this fact disturbs Isabella more and more. It gives a dark edge to the crisp and sunny winter days, a darkness embodied in the powerful trunks of the trees protecting the cottage and yet also making it vulnerable to whatever might be hiding in the forest.

She sets the bucket down on the edge of the well and rests for a moment, taking a deep breath of the sharp cold air.

She still does not know how she got here. Carol simply refuses to tell her, very kindly but firmly, and she cannot bring herself to insist, not when the old woman is being so kind to her. And the truth is, part of her does not want to know, not yet, because it enables her to cherish the hope it was Bernard who rescued her from his sister's clutches. The last thing she remembers is begging Rose to tell him what Bridget was doing to her, and now here she is.

She cannot stop thinking about Lord Wulvedon. She thinks about him more than she thinks about what she endured on the 'tree', and very often the line between her two obsessions blurs and her feelings cannot tell the difference between them. It seems there really is something to his seductive ideas of pain, and this gives a frightening credibility to the fact that he always wears black just like a priest, but without the pure white collar around his throat. She knows this is a terribly sacrilegious thought, but she cannot help it… Lord Wulvedon, who so generously accepted her wordless confession when she thrust her tongue eagerly into his mouth because it helped her

176

understand things so much more clearly than words ever had… Lord Wulvedon, who spread her thighs and nailed her down on the crypt, making her bleed around him, nothing like the old priest in the humble little church where she attended mass her whole life holding up the chalice as he said in a weak, bored voice, '*This is my blood*…'

'Isabella,' Carol pops her head around the door, 'I need that water now, dear.'

'Yes, I am coming.' She picks the bucket up by the handle and carries it carefully into the cottage, which seems darker than it really is after the glare of sunlight reflecting off snow. 'Do you need more?'

'No, that is good enough for now, thank you, dear.' Carol is preparing yet another one of her delicious stews.

'Then if you do not need anything, I think I will go for a little walk.'

'In this weather? You will catch your death,' Carol declares, but there is no real objection in her tone.

'It is perfectly lovely out.'

'Maybe to your young bones.' She sighs, and then adds sternly, 'Very well, but do not stray too far, Isabella, there may be wolves about.'

'I will be back shortly,' she promises, and turns quickly away from her recurring dream of fires burning in the night and black wolves feasting between the thighs of helpless girls moaning and writhing in mingled pain and ecstasy…

It is a relief to be back outside. The air is sharp and cold as the edge of a blade cutting through her thoughts and allowing her to simply enjoy the sense of her freedom. She gleaned from Carol's expression as the old woman helped her bathe one night, that the back of her body is a landscape of darkening welts, yet they do not hurt at all anymore. She finds it wonderfully invigorating not to be

177

locked up in a windowless room, as she was at the Castle. She has never felt stronger, and picking up her plain gray skirt, she heads confidently away from the cottage.

Whoever carried her here also brought her trunk, so she has all her books and dresses, at least the few not ruined at the Castle, one way or another. She is wearing her gray wool cloak today, with gray gloves and fur-lined black boots. The thin layer of snow on the ground has hardened into ice, which cracks beneath her every step and keeps her attention sharp while underscoring the profound silence of the world around her. The woods seem to be lifeless; they are so still and empty of anything except bare branches. She wonders in which direction the Castle lies and how far away it is, grateful she has been granted a reprieve from all her worries for a little while. She has no money, but when she said as much to Carol, the old woman bluntly told her she had already been paid much more than was necessary to take care of her, and that she would have done so whether she was paid or not, so she did not want to hear another word about it.

Isabella's heart feels lighter and more hopeful the faster and farther she walks along the edge of the forest. She is tempted to enter it and see where the winding path between the trees leads her, but she is afraid of becoming lost. She grew up in the middle of a city and finds nature's unrestrained power much too awe inspiring not to respect it… as she respects Lord Wulvedon… as she is excited by him and yet also frightened of him…

She pauses when she hears a sound distinct from the crunching of icy snow beneath her feet. She stands there listening, and a faint thundering rumble reaches her ears. It is mid-afternoon. Perhaps another storm is brewing somewhere behind the trees. Or it could be she is near a road and is hearing a group of horses harnessed to a carriage galloping by. Yet the sound only grows louder and more distinct, and seems to be coming from behind her…

She turns back in the direction of the cottage.

Three large black horses are riding towards her, the black capes of the riders billowing behind them like demonic wings, and they are clearly following the trail of her footprints.

Isabella turns around again and runs into the woods, but the bare branches are high above her; there is enough room between the trees for the horses to follow if they want to, and a quick glance over her shoulder tells her that they do indeed want to.

She stops and leans back against a trunk. There is no point in running any farther. She will only be weaker and more breathless when they finally catch her, and they will be angry with her for forcing them to lead their beautiful, expensive mounts onto ground treacherous with roots on which one of them might break a leg. So she waits tensely for the riders to rein in around her. She relaxes slightly when she recognizes Matthew, followed by the younger man who blindfolded her before leading her down to Lord Wulvedon's dungeon. Then she looks up at the third rider. 'My lord!' she gasps.

'You have caused quite a problem for me, Isabella,' Bernard says quietly.

'I am sorry,' she whispers, and then wonders why the devil she is the one apologizing after everything he has done to her.

His dark eyes stare intently down into hers. 'I see you are feeling better.'

'Yes, my lord, thank you.' Too late, she remembers what he said the last time she thanked him, and it seems she is still in a dangerous position, perhaps more dangerous than ever.

'I understand my sister nearly killed you.' Yet he looks angrily down at her as if it is *her* fault for leading Bridget into such a sinful temptation.

'Then Rose told you?'

'Rose?'

'I asked her to go to you and—'

'Rose never came to me and told me anything.' He tugs viciously on his horse's bit to hold him still.

'Then you did not…? Then it was not you who…?'

Mathew abruptly joins the conversation. 'It was Lady Wulvedon who had you brought here when she realized her mistake.'

Isabella assimilates what he is saying even as she cannot take her eyes off Lord Wulvedon, still unable to believe the cold-blooded truth even as it stares her directly in the face. 'Then… then you really do not care,' she concludes miserably.

He dismounts abruptly.

She looks wildly around her, but the broad trunk behind her and his two men on horseback before her have her fenced in. The only place she can take refuge as he walks right up to her is his eyes, where she lets go of everything, all her fears as well as all her hopes, and plunges into their stormy depths.

He catches her by the arms. 'I just got back, Isabella,' he says furiously.

'You just got back?' she repeats hopefully.

'Yes!' He shakes her as if this will help her think more clearly. But then, as if he knows this will not be enough, he pulls her against him and begins kissing her, thrusting his tongue into her mouth as if to forcibly rearrange all her perceptions and feelings more sensibly inside her.

Matthew clears his throat. 'My lord…'

Bernard turns his face away from hers just far enough to snap, 'What?'

'Are you sure?'

Lord Wulvedon gazes down at Isabella's closed eyes, at her long black lashes fluttering slightly against her pale cheeks and at her moist, parted lips waiting for his kiss like a baby bird helplessly starved for his tongue. 'Yes,' he says, sounding immensely relieved. 'Yes!' he sighs.

'Well, I hope so, because there will be hell to pay.'

'But there is divine justice in that, Matthew; Fate is having fun with me.'

'It is not Fate I am worried about.'

Isabella moans and opens her eyes, impatient of all this talk when she and Lord Wulvedon were sharing something much more vital.

He smiles at her suddenly, that clean, wolf-like grin of his that makes her weak in the knees, so they bend easily when he puts his hands on her shoulders and forces her down before him. The white sheet of snow cracks beneath her, but she scarcely notices as she reaches into his cape, where she is thrilled to discover his gloved hands already busy unbuttoning his leggings. She waits impatiently, caressing the firm bulge beneath the prize he is unwrapping for her while staring worshipfully up at his face. His smile vanishes as with one hand he tents her beneath his cloak, while with the other he grabs her by the hair and swiftly forces her face down over his erection.

She moans in ecstasy, cloaked in a warm darkness that smells and tastes and feels of nothing except Lord Wulvedon. She longs to swallow his entire hardening shaft the way Juliet did, but whenever the engorged tip strokes the sensitive space at the back of her mouth her chest heaves and she nearly gags. Yet she is desperate for all of him, not just to prove she can please him as well, or better, than any other girl, but because she is so hungry for him she feels it is going to kill her if she cannot put all of him in her mouth. Which is why when he grabs her head with both hands she is glad, because it means he senses how much she wants all of him and is going to make her take all of him.

She braces herself on his thighs the way she saw Juliet do as he leans over her, tilting her head back slightly as he selfishly seeks the inexpressibly delicious caress of her throat.

The darkness inside his cloak deepens and grows hotter, becoming a breathless torment for her, but she remembers what she learned hanging from the 'tree' – the secret of relaxing rather than tensing, of anticipating and accepting instead of dreading and fighting – and her reward is the excruciating yet highly gratifying experience of making it possible for her lord to sheathe his entire penis in the vulnerable length of her throat. The satisfaction she takes in his total penetration transcends the supreme discomfort, even when he begins moving his hips back and forth, gently but relentlessly. He must know the violent effort it costs her not to gag on him, but he also seems aware that the more she suffers to please him the more she perversely longs to continue suffering and pleasing him.

And when he groans, tightening his grip on her head, all her efforts are rewarded. It does not matter she can scarcely breathe, since his approval is as important as air to her.

'Oh, Isabella…' He sounds impossibly weak, as if he is willingly sacrificing himself to her bottomless hunger.

She moans in response, digging her fingers into his thighs, remembering the ghostly milk spurting out of him in a dark crypt as she feels it flowing down the dark shaft of her throat. She is almost afraid his body will collapse over her face as she senses his soul rising beyond her for a few terribly arduous moments, in which he leaves only his stiff flesh buried inside her.

# Chapter Twelve

Isabella discovers she is not very good at waiting. In fact, she very much hates waiting. It creates a gap between the past and the future into which all sorts of doubts crawl like bugs between the floorboards. Lord Wulvedon promised he would send for her, three days ago. He spoke the words, 'I will send for you, Isabella,' three infinitely long days and nights ago.

'Good heavens, child,' Carol lets her constantly working hands rest for a moment, 'you remind me of a fly trapped in a jar.'

'I am sorry.' She thrusts the poker into the fire to create another gratifyingly restless shower of sparks. 'But tomorrow is Christmas Eve,' she announces, as if this explains her growing tension. And maybe it does, because part of her cannot believe she is actually going to get what she wants.

'Yes, I know, dear.' The old woman's voice softens. 'It will be the first Christmas you spend without your father.'

'Yes.' But the truth is she is not thinking about her father, or about the heavenly Father and his Son. She is thinking about a sinful, sadistic nobleman.

'I will be making a special minced meat pie to celebrate.'

'Mm.' Isabella's lips tighten in a frown as she kneels on the warm hearthstones, staring into the flames. She is not interested in food. She is not interested in anything except whether or not Lord Wulvedon intends to keep his promise. If he does indeed send for her as he said he would, then she will care about everything else again, which means that in a very real sense he will be giving her the world for Christmas. If he is lying, however, and he does not really plan to send for her at all…

'Isabella, if you get any closer to the fire you are going to fall in, and I will have only your ashes to give to Lord Wulvedon's men when they come for you.'

She smiles over her shoulder at Carol, and wonders if the woman is too old to remember what it is like to feel as though you are burning up inside, whether close to a fire or not. 'Then you think they *will* come?' She hates how doubtful she sounds, but she cannot help it.

'Nothing is certain in this world, dear, but if Lord Wulvedon said he would send for you, then he will most certainly send for you.'

Isabella's shoulders sag with relief, because it is a terrible strain on her to question Bernard's word. It fills her with a despair kin to the world being proved to be nothing but a mere coincidence of chemicals. 'Carol,' she rises, abruptly realizing how dark and chilly the little cottage is as she turns towards her patient hostess, 'why did Lady Wulvedon bring me here?' Unbelievably, it did not occur to her until now to wonder why her tormenter simply did not have someone at the Castle nurse her wounds.

Carol keeps her eyes on her knitting. 'I suspect she wanted you as far away as possible,' she mutters.

'As far away as possible from what?' It could not have been from her brother, for Bernard had been gone the whole time.

'As far away from *her* as possible, Isabella.' Carol's eyes meets her eyes, and the shadows flickering across her wrinkled face make it look at least a century old. She does not need to speak for the young girl to hear what she is thinking, because Isabella can scarcely believe herself how much she longs to return to the Castle. Yet she has no choice. If she wants to be with Bernard she not only has to go back to the Castle, she must live there and call it home.

She avoids this thought by asking again, 'But why did she bring me *here*, Carol?'

'Because she knew I would care for you as my own. You see,' she returns patiently to her work, 'I was her nanny.'

She finds it nearly impossible to picture the beautifully vicious Bridget as an innocent little baby resting where a pile of golden yarn now lies.

'I suppose you know she and Bernard are twins,' Carol goes on comfortably, 'and so, naturally, I cared for them both.'

'You were Bernard's nanny, too?'

'And his wet-nurse. He suckled at my breasts.'

She experiences an irrational stab of jealousy gazing at Carol's full but sagging bosom as the old woman glances at her with a satisfied little smirk, making her blush. Turning away, she walks over to the bed and seats herself restlessly on its edge.

'My dear,' Carol lays her knitting aside, 'you are like a sparrow fallen into a falcon's nest. Do you have any idea what you are getting yourself into by allowing yourself to fall in love with this man?' She folds her gnarled but still nimble hands in her lap. She is holding Isabella's heartstrings now instead of her copper knitting needles, waiting patiently for her to begin unraveling all her passionately tangled feelings.

'I have not,' she clenches her smooth young hands in her own lap, '*allowed* myself to fall in love, it just—'

'Happened. Yes, I know.'

'Love is not a hole in the ground you just fall into,' she

remembers Bridget's analogy, 'but it is not something you can control with your mind, either.'

The old woman laughs and begins rocking back and forth slowly. 'No, you most certainly cannot control it,' she agrees comfortably, 'and not all fires lend themselves to a cozy hearth. Some are destructively violent, some are mere physical sparks, some die out once the illusion that kindled them proves to be made of ashes, like everyone, and a few burn steadily and beautifully and are still going strong even when the bodies enjoying this divine warmth finally wear out. The question is, what is the nature of the love you feel for this man?'

Isabella has to admit it is violent, but that does not necessarily mean it is destructive, and as for a cozy hearth, the Castle's fireplaces are large enough to accommodate the blaze of feeling inside her whenever she thinks about Lord Wulvedon. What she feels for him is more than just physical attraction even though she knows very well what he is like, and she can easily imagine the intense desires he inspires in her on all levels of her being surviving death... 'It is my soul that loves his,' she concludes quietly. 'My mind, my heart and my body can do nothing about it. They can only obey how my soul feels about him because it is everything.'

Carol nods, not appearing at all surprised by the cryptic response. 'For years Lord Wulvedon has been searching high and low for the other half of his soul, Isabella. Every autumn he ravages the countryside, harvesting all the beautiful young maidens for himself. He shoves them in his basement like grain and sees what they are made of in the heat of suffering and pain, waiting for one of them to rise to the challenge and capture his heart with the fullness of her beauty, inside and out. He pours their feelings for himself like wine, enjoys the bouquet of their souls, and hopes one of them will succeed in intoxicating him. You are the only one who has ever made him lose his head, Isabella.'

She savors this wonderful fact for a moment, but it leaves a bitter aftertaste, which prompts her to ask, 'But what happens to all the other girls?'

'That is up to them.'

'What do you mean? Do they remain at the Castle?' She thinks about Bridget referring to her girls as property. 'Do they remain at the Castle as his... as his *slaves?*'

'If that is what they wish,' the old woman blithely confirms her worst fear.

'How could anyone wish that?' She rises in indignation, but there is nowhere to go so she sits back down on the bed again. 'How can any girl wish to belong to a man who does not care for her?'

'The fact that he does not love them does not mean he does not care for them. You see, Isabella, not everyone's needs are the same. Many of the girls who accept the *Message* when it comes do so because their deepest desire is to escape a life of hardship and poverty, because they dream of a life of luxury and ease, and to this end they do their best to seduce Lord Wulvedon and win his heart. Oh, some of them may also be searching for love or believe they are, and if it is love they truly want, then they set themselves free in the end. But most of the girls who suffer the torments of the Castle do so from a lust for wealth and power. Bernard was searching for a rare jewel in a collection of fortune hunters.'

'But what do you mean, that what happens to them is what they wish?'

Carol laughs again. 'You are relentless. No wonder he likes you. Different things happen to them, it all depends on them or, I dare say, on his mood at the time.'

Isabella thinks of the stone altar in the torch-lit dungeon and of the long, deadly daggers so casually worn by his men. 'Oh my God,' she whispers.

'Whatever you are thinking do not be ridiculous, dear, but you are walking on the edge of a sword here. Lord and Lady Wulvedon have been inseparable since before they were born. They shared the same womb and now...' She shakes her head.

'What?' Isabella asks tensely. 'I have no desire to come between them. I tried to be Bridget's friend, but... but she made it impossible. She kept insisting my preference for men was only something I had been taught, but she was wrong. How I feel about her brother is... well, it is everything.'

'Yes, I know, dear. Unfortunately, Bridget feels the same way,' she reaches for her knitting again, 'about you.'

The package arrives at sunrise. Carol is already up and about and opens the front door.

Isabella sits up in bed appalled by the thought of Bernard seeing her like this, all puffy-eyed and with a pillow-creased cheek and stray wisps of hair escaping her braid.

The old woman steps aside, and one of Lord Wulvedon's men enters the cottage, immediately making it feel even smaller and poorer compared to the rich gleam of his black leather cape and boots. He seems careful not to look at the young woman on the bed as he sets a bundle down on a table beneath the window. Whatever it is he has brought her, it is neatly wrapped in a white cloth with a silver border that catches the light of the rising sun.

Isabella blinks against the golden glow reflecting off the snow as Carol holds the door open for the messenger from the Castle, who nods politely to her on his way out. The second he is gone, she gets out of bed. She is still fully clothed in her plainest gray dress because it gets cold in the little house at night when the fire inevitably dies down, and she rushes over to the package in her stocking feet.

'Lord Wulvedon will be sending for you today,' Carol informs her, as she returns to the task of baking bread for breakfast.

Isabella knows before she even touches it that the bundle contains a dress, and two firm lumps on top seem to indicate the presence of shoes, as well as something else.

It takes all the patience she possesses to open her gift slowly and carefully. Even the silver-trimmed cloth in which it is wrapped is finer than anything she owns.

There turn out to be six different parts to the gift, and all of them leave her speechless for one reason or another.

The shoes have heels long and sharp enough to draw blood, which is the color of their satin cloth. She has no idea how she will be able to walk in them, yet they are exquisite in a daunting way. She sets them down side-by-side on the floor, impressed by Lord Wulvedon's powers of observation, because they appear to be exactly her size and she never noticed him looking at her feet.

The white stockings are such a sheer wonder everything poses a threat to them – the rough edge of the table, even her own fingernails – so she lays them carefully across the bed before proceeding to examine what lay beneath them. It is a corset, the same shocking red color as the shoes, and like the stockings it serves no practical purpose she can see as it will barely cover her bosom. It will, however, serve to push her breasts up and press them together in a provocative way considering the plunging neckline of the white gown she will be wearing over it. Standing with her back to the window, she holds the long dress up in front of her, and her breath catches. The morning light makes the dozens of pearls sewn into the satin cloth glimmer as if still wet from the sea where they were formed inside rough dark shells.

'Oh my word,' Carol exclaims, 'it is a wedding dress!'

Isabella lays the gown reverently across the bed beside the stockings, but she does not let herself think about it, not yet. Fortunately, there are more items in the package to distract her – a long, fur-lined red cloak folded around a pair of matching elbow-length gloves, and a narrow black box.

She has never actually touched rubies before, and the choker of red roses in full bloom is by far the most beautiful thing she has ever seen in her life.

'Well, well, well,' Carol says quietly, 'it is a pleasure to meet you, my lady.'

The carriage arrives at dusk. Perched on the edge of the bed, Isabella hears it pull up. The thunder of hooves muffled by falling snow and the rush of wheels all feel as though they are happening inside her rather than in the yard outside. Her heart starts racing so she cannot seem to take a deep breath, and the fact she can scarcely walk in the red shoes she is wearing makes her even more nervous. She cannot believe what is happening. What *is* happening? All she knows is she longs to be with Lord Wulvedon, but how this desire can translate into reality is a complete mystery to her.

'Come, Isabella, it is time,' Carol urges gently.

'But I will trip over myself in these shoes,' she glances down at her impossibly deep cleavage, 'and I feel imprisoned in this corset, and the little clasps keep snapping off the stockings I am so afraid of tearing, and—'

'Good heavens, child, relax. I wish I had a mirror. If you knew what Lord Wulvedon will see when he looks at you, you would understand that all these little discomforts are a very small price to pay for the power you will have over him.'

'But these are all *his* gifts.'

'Which means he *wants* you to have power over him. Do not be afraid. Those shoes, that dress, the rubies around your neck, they are all weapons you have won for yourself by the sheer force of your personality and the magic of your beauty. Do not hesitate to use them to attain your heart's desire. If you do not, when you are an old woman like me you will deeply regret wasting these gifts from Lord Wulvedon and from God.'

Isabella rises, and Carol's words somehow help her balance on the red shoes' stiletto heels. She holds the gown's full white skirt up beneath the red cloak she has on over it, and walks carefully across the uneven wooden floorboards towards the front door. It opens abruptly, admitting a veil of snowflakes carried in on a freezing gust of wind, and two men in glistening black capes and boots.

'My lady,' they each sink to one knee before her, lowering their heads as though worshipping a statue of the virgin in church.

'Good evening,' she replies, glancing desperately at Carol, who merely shrugs and smiles. 'Um… I am ready.'

As though her words release them from a spell, they rise in unison and one of them hands Carol a small green-velvet purse. 'For your trouble,' he says respectfully.

'She was no trouble at all,' the old woman replies placidly. 'I shall miss her.'

Isabella has a brilliant idea. 'Can you not come with us, Carol?'

'No, dear, but I do hope you will visit me every now and then.'

'Of course I will.' She suddenly has no desire to leave the cozy little cottage.

As though sensing her hesitation, the second man smiles at her, tosses his cape over one shoulder, and lifts her gently up into his arms.

Isabella slips her own arms comfortably around his neck and returns his smile, grateful she will not have to walk through the snow in the dangerously beautiful shoes.

'Remember yourself,' Carol urges as Lord Wulvedon's man carries Isabella through the door, at which point she is very glad of her fur-lined cloak. It has been snowing since early afternoon, and now the sun has almost set it is even colder outside. The wind also feels stronger, emboldening the ghostly flakes, which seem to fall faster and harder now their warm and luminous enemy is surrendering for the night.

The carriage door is opened and she is set down inside the frigid little compartment. She is left alone in the dark, rubbing her gloved hands together and shivering, with anticipation more than anything. She cannot imagine what sort of reception awaits her at the Castle. She cherishes the hope she will be taken directly to Bernard's quarters, where she will be alone with him for the first time ever, yet part of her knows very well this pleasant fantasy is not going to happen, at least not yet. None of her experiences on the Wulvedon Estate were ever so easy, and there is no reason to believe that will change now.

The carriage rocks gently on its way, its progress made eerily silent by the soft new snow covering the icy layer beneath it. Isabella's hand rises to her throat and the rubies encircling it. The precious stones were cold when they lay inside their little black box, but their fiery depths have absorbed the warmth of her flesh. She is not anxious about the weather making travel by night dangerous; she is confident Lord Wulvedon's men will deliver her to him safely. It is what awaits her inside the Castle's luxuriously comfortable interior that worries her. There are too many things she does not wish to think about. Yet in the gently rocking darkness there is no hiding from all the questions that have their hooks in her soul, even as she cannot also help but be stimulatingly aware of her body beneath the cloak. The ermine lining caresses her chest and her bosom, which she is afraid will swell right out of the corset with every deep breath she takes to try and soothe her nerves. The little hooks dangling from it and holding up her stockings are insistently cold against her thighs, the tops of which are as bare as her bottom. The pearl-studded dress is cool and soft against her legs, and the deep space between her thighs has no problem staying warm. Her pussy has been smoldering all day, its mysteriously wet heat stoked by her constant thoughts of Lord Wulvedon, and by wondering just what he plans to do with her.

And what is *she* going to do about all those other girls? Although perhaps the question she should be asking herself is '*Can* I do anything about all those other girls?' And what on earth is she going to do about Lady Wulvedon? If Carol is right and Bridget feels about her as she does about her brother… the mere thought creates a storm of feelings inside her, which makes it impossible for her to think clearly just as night and snow falling together make it difficult for her escorts to see where they are going. And yet, unbelievable as it seems, she is no longer afraid of Lady Wulvedon. It is not because she is sure that in the future Bernard will protect her from his sister. Perhaps it has something to do with having been called 'lady' herself three times today already, and three is a charm putting her on equal footing with Bridget. Take away the difference in their social status and Isabella can admit she feels superior to Bernard's beautiful sister in many subtle and vital ways. She survived the torments of the 'tree' without succumbing to Bridget's demands that she repent her actions. She won.

She shivers and hugs herself beneath the cloak. It is Christmas Eve. She wonders if the Castle has its own private chapel and if they will hold a Midnight Mass there. One of her fondest memories is standing in the doorway of the little church she and her father always attended – because it was always standing room only on Christmas Eve – feeling the cold wind on her back and glancing over her shoulder to watch the snow falling from the black sky, and then looking back into the church, warm with hundreds of bodies and from all the candlelight sparkling off the priest's gilded vestments…

She returns to the present with a jolt as the carriage comes to an abrupt stop. She holds her breath, waiting for it to continue on its way, which it does a moment later. The large wheels must have encountered a root or a fallen branch buried beneath the fresh snow.

This is not going to be any normal Christmas Eve, she can be sure of that.


Isabella knows they have arrived at their destination when the carriage's rocking motion gradually ceases. Her door opens almost immediately, and once again she is cradled in a strong pair of arms carrying her across torch-lit snow. She blinks snowflakes out of her eyes as she gazes up at the Castle's dark walls. They loom over her, ominous and forbidding, and they feel like home.

Lord Wulvedon's man crosses the courtyard with her and carries her through a pair of double doors, which open for them as if by magic. They close again in the same silent and inexorable fashion as he sets her down.

She glimpses two figures slipping furtively back into the shadows, and wonders at the effort being made to produce the impression of supernatural motion even as she appreciates it. The effect is thrilling, and gives her the idea of adopting the same attitude towards the crippling heels she is expected to walk on gracefully.

Lord Wulvedon's man steps behind her and relieves her of her damp cloak, exposing her pearl-encrusted gown, but he does not ask for her gloves, so she keeps them on. Carol took a great deal of time arranging her hair, gathering part of it up and allowing the rest to tumble down around her face and over her shoulders in lovely ringlets.

'This way, my lady.' He precedes her across the polished black floor fervently licked by long and agile tongues of torchlight, which do nothing to warm its cold stone heart.

It does not even occur to her to ask him where they are going. She has learned to accept the Castle's inexorable laws. The important thing is Lord Wulvedon has sent for her and is waiting for her.

Her guide pushes open another pair of doors and steps aside to let her pass.

The chamber she enters makes her think of all the great Cathedrals she has read about. Arched beams soar high above her head, thousands of candles burn in sconces on the walls and in beautiful bush-like chandeliers, and the rich red and gold color of the arches is reflected everywhere below them – in the wax melting over gilded candelabra, in the rug covering the entire floor, and in the heavy drapes keeping out the damp and the cold whilst outlining Lord Wulvedon's black-clad figure for her with stunning clarity.

He is standing directly across from her at the opposite end of the opulent space, alone on a dais, a straight path leading to him formed by a splendid congregation of men and women.

At that moment something happens inside Isabella. Even as part of her begins to panic feeling the attention of so many people focused entirely on her, her body begins walking calmly and purposefully towards Lord Wulvedon. She has nothing to be ashamed of, and with his direct stare essentially pulling her to him, it is easy to forget there is anyone else in the room since nothing matters as much as her irresistible attraction to him. The corners of her eyes awash with colors and textures and the unmistakably deep glimmer of gemstones, she feels as though she has stepped into a tapestry – into a fabled kingdom that has conquered the proverbial Dragon whose vast serpentine body she is walking across in the rug's red and gold spirals.

Lady Wulvedon is standing at the head of the line to the left. Her hair is pulled severely back from her face in her preferred style, and she is wearing yet another formfitting black gown with detached glove-like sleeves, only this particular dress is cut into the shape of an X, exposing more of her body than it conceals. The design almost strikes Isabella as a divine mockery, as if after God fashioned her body He drew a big X over it because he was dissatisfied with his work, which nevertheless is as close to perfection as a mortal woman can get.

Then her awareness of Bridget and of everything else slips away when Lord Wulvedon holds out his hand to her.

'Isabella.' His deep voice steadies her nerves as she ascends the six gilded steps separating them, and slips her red-gloved fingers into his black ones. He smiles down at her for an instant, and then looks over at his sister. 'Bridget!'

As she turns to face the room with him, Isabella is very

glad he did not say *her* name that way.

Lady Wulvedon approaches the foot of the steps. Above the thin red gash of her mouth her eyes are big and soft and uncertain. 'My lord,' she replies quietly.

'You have abused your power, sister,' Lord Wulvedon's voice carries effortlessly across the chamber, 'and for that you must be punished. Are you prepared to suffer the consequences of your actions?'

Bridget holds her head high as she answers, 'Yes, my lord, I am prepared.'

'Then Isabella will decide what your punishment shall be.'

All eyes come to rest on her again. She feels their touch like live flames, and for a moment everyone's attention focused on her again blinds her so she cannot see her thoughts to make any sense of them, much less speak.

Lord Wulvedon gives her hand a hard, encouraging squeeze.

'I understand, my lady,' she begins, concentrating on Bridget's chiseled features, which give nothing away except the superficial fact of their loveliness, 'you desired something from me I could not give you.' She glances at Bernard's stern profile.

'Speak so everyone can hear you, Isabella,' he instructs. Then he announces in his deep, forceful tone, 'My sister violated two of the most important laws we live by; that a slave must consent to his or her slavery, and that a slave must never be forced to endure more pain than he or she has the ability to transform into pleasure. When a master or a mistress endangers a slave's life by losing control, a sacred trust is betrayed, and any violation of this trust, when one person puts their life in the hands of another, must be punished as an example to anyone else who might be tempted to violate the integrity of this bond.'

'Thank you,' Isabella whispers fervently, for the information, which gives her some idea of how to proceed, for the help she is now sure he would have given her had he known what she was being made to suffer, but especially for his profoundly ethical approach to matters that on the surface appear to be totally sinful and lacking in any profound sense of morality.

'I made it clear to Lady Wulvedon from the very beginning,' she goes on in a clear voice, given confidence by the uncompromising strength of Lord Wulvedon's grasp, 'at least from the moment I understood what was expected of me here, that I wished to serve her brother, not her. Yet she insisted I felt this way because I had been raised to think I desired men over women. I appreciate that she was convinced of this herself, yet I do not believe she refused to take "no" for an answer because she was interested in my welfare. I believe, my lady,' she looks directly at Bridget, 'you knew from the moment I said I wished to serve your brother that it was true, and that the urge came directly from my soul and not from my mind, which is the only part of us subject to the opinions and perspectives of others. I say your crime was to deliberately defy a metaphysical reality, which for you became embodied in me and in my feelings for your brother. You beat me because you could not face the truth I could never feel about you the way I feel about Bernard. Yet because I understand what you are going through and how much it hurts, I cannot punish you for what you did to me. You are suffering enough.'

A ripple of surprise animates the icon-like gathering.

'However,' Isabella goes on firmly, 'there was no reason for you to deny me access to the library. As your tutor, I not only had every right to see it, I should have been permitted to spend as much time there as I wished. But instead you repeatedly refused to let me see the library, and for this senseless cruelty I cannot possibly forgive you. My lord, please have your sister taken to the *tree*.'

# Chapter Thirteen

Bridget's full breasts quiver with every lash of the whip across her back. It was an easy matter for Lord Wulvedon's men to slice open the cloth X barely covering her torso, especially since she did nothing to try and stop them. At first Matthew and two other men – whose names Isabella still does not know but whose faces and figures she recognizes quite well by now – hesitated to approach Bernard's heretofore untouchable sister, but one uncertain glance at Lord Wulvedon and his new lady promptly cured them of their hesitation and left only their lust.

Isabella is finding it a bit difficult to admit to herself how much it excites her to watch Bernard's sister beaten on her command. *She is* responsible for this beautiful woman's pain and humiliation, a fact that should make her feel profoundly ashamed of herself, but which instead has the opposite effect. She loves every violent second so much, she orders Lord Wulvedon's man to stop for a moment so she can more fully savor the pleasure she takes in the sadistic scene.

Matthew obligingly lets the whip fall to his side and smiles at her where she stands beside Lord Wulvedon, a half empty glass of red wine in her hand, which Rose takes it upon herself to refill.

'Thank you.' She smiles at the other girl, who avoids her eyes. For a fleetingly wicked moment, Isabella considers having Lady Wulvedon's girls all punished with her, but the temptation passes, mainly because she knows it will dilute the experience of watching Bridget suffer.

'Would you like to sit down?' Bernard asks her.

'No, thank you, my lord, I would prefer to stand.' She nods at Matthew, and he promptly whips Lady Wulvedon across the back again.

Bridget gasps beneath the impact, but still refuses to cry out. Her long hair has been pinned up out of the way, and Isabella finds the sight of the pole thrusting up between her full breasts very arousing, which is why she prefers to stand, so she can move around the 'tree' and enjoy every angle of Bridget's chained and suspended body.

Only a fraction of all the splendidly dressed persons gathered in the red and gold hall accompanied them here to Lady Wulvedon's quarters. Isabella has no idea where the rest of them went as she looks around her at the select few enjoying the entertainment she, unbelievably, is providing for them. Three couples occupy the jewel-colored divans from which Rose and Elaine watched her being caned, and a group of six lovely girls is reclining on cushions near the 'tree', their eyes fixed hungrily on Bridget.

'Who are these people, my lord?' she asks.

'Oh, just some old friends,' he replies casually, 'and ex slaves.'

She looks up at him. 'Ex *slaves?*'

'Well,' he smiles down at her, 'they still *are* slaves, they simply belong to a new master. You see, my lady,' he traces one of her cheekbones with his fingertips, 'I not only grow wine and breed cattle, I also cultivate another highly prized commodity.'

'Slaves,' she repeats flatly.

His smile deepens and he kisses her forehead as if the gentle pressure of his lips will better help her absorb the shocking statement. 'Yes, Isabella, beautiful and exquisitely submissive women. My sister and I break them in, then train them and enjoy them until such time as they desire to leave, either on their own or as another master or mistress's prized possession.'

'They choose to remain slaves all their lives?' Incredulity distracts her from Bridget's punishment. She raises her hand, and Matthew pauses again.

Lord Wulvedon takes a sip of wine before replying, looking deeply into her eyes. 'Is that not what you have chosen for yourself, Isabella?'

'Yes,' she says without hesitation, 'I wish to serve you forever, my lord, because I love you more than anything.'

His stare hardening, he tenderly cradles one of her cheeks in his free hand.

She turns her face and gives his palm a worshipful kiss before resting the full weight of her head in his hand for a wonderful moment.

'I suggest you enjoy your brief taste of domination while it lasts, my love, for I have other plans for you later.'

It is both a threat and a promise, and his tone rouses her from her romantic reverie. 'What sort of plans, my lord?'

He looks away. 'That is for me to know,' he sips his wine again, 'and for you to find out.'

For some reason, his response fills her with an inexpressible happiness. Up until then she allowed Bridget to keep her skirt, but now a gesture from her directed at one of Lord Wulvedon's men quickly relieves Bernard's sister of the black cloth concealing her long legs.

Lady Wulvedon is wearing a black lace garter belt around her waist, black stockings and black high heels. She has a boy's tight little bottom and narrow hips.

'I think it is time for the cane,' Isabella announces.

Matthew hands the whip over to another man and exchanges it for a slender bamboo rod.

Even with her body stretched taut and her wrists bound over her head, Bridget visibly tenses. She stared impassively into space as she was whipped, but now her eyes close.

Isabella understands; it requires a great deal of concentration to endure the agony inflicted by the cane. 'Wait,' she says abruptly, 'this is much too easy for her. Take her down, please, and *you*,' she addresses a young man hovering nearby, 'lie on the floor and make her sit on you. And *you* kneel in front of her and put your penis in her mouth. Then, Matthew, you may proceed.'

'No!' Bridget cries as her wrists are freed. 'No!'

Isabella answers her furious glance with a smile. 'I am being kind,' she explains graciously. 'A real erection feels much better than a big ivory penis like the one with which you sought to deflower me. Fortunately for me, and for you now, your brother got there first.'

Bridget gives her another tight-lipped glare as two men hold her still while a third spreads himself on his back in front of her and quickly unbuttons his leggings. His erection springs up tall and proud and Isabella studies it curiously. It is more slender than Lord Wulvedon's, curving slightly, and the head is quite distinct from the shaft, making her think of a mushroom cap. Lady Wulvedon is made to stand directly over it, her sharp heels planted on either side of his hips, and then four hands pushing down on her shoulders force her to bend her knees until the lips of her sex enfold the tip of the cock pushing eagerly up into her pussy. 'No!' she gasps as the man beneath her grabs her by the waist and pulls her down on top of him, groaning as his cock surges deep into her belly.

Isabella completely forgets about the glass of wine in her hand, watching Lady Wulvedon's hair escape the pins restraining it as a second man abruptly grips her chin and forces her to face another rampant penis seeking an entrance into her highly desirable body. He feeds himself into her mouth with brave determination, but unfortunately Isabella cannot see her expression as he does so because his large gloved hands consume Bridget's face like two black spiders. He holds her head as though he has every right to it, as though it was made for him, and Lady Wulvedon is very gratifyingly trapped between two men making selfish use of two of her available orifices. The dick stroking itself with her lips also gets to enjoy the subtle caress of her moans, which become even more intensely pleasurable when Matthew steps up behind her, and cracks the cane viciously across her back. He delivers the blow so the pain penetrates her in time with the men, making it impossible for her to scream or flinch beneath the excruciating sensation. He brings the cane down again as she clings to the hips of the man penetrating her mouth, and the welts rising on her fine skin make Isabella think of a bas-relief, and then of a fresco in the haunting ruins of Pompeii where a woman kneels with her head in a man's lap, her toga draped around her knees as she submits to a scared beating.

Matthew continues carving brutally exciting paths across Lady Wulvedon's back that all lead to Isabella's revenge. Yet what arouses her more than anything is the vision of two men forcing Bridget to serve them.

'Would you like that done to you?' Lord Wulvedon whispers in her ear.

Isabella is afraid to answer. She is not sure she would, but she is not entirely sure she would not. Very different rules of logic rule at the Castle, where reason twists in on itself like the mystical snake swallowing its tail. *Reward* and *punishment*, there seems no distinguishing between them. 'Yes, my lord,' she replies at last, 'if it would please you, because you are the only man I truly desire inside me. And yet,' doubts assail her soul as painfully as a cane striking her flesh, 'how can you say you love me if you are willing to share me with other men?' She looks away in growing despair. 'And if I am forced to share you with other women?'

'Look at me,' he commands gently, and waits for her to obey him before continuing. 'It is all about us, now and always. What we have, what we feel for each other, is mysteriously special, and you know it. But other people can serve as exciting sensual extensions of our love for each other, Isabella. They can intensify our intimacy by enhancing our ability to arouse and please each other. Yet it will always be about us,' he repeats firmly. 'Never doubt that. I searched a long time for you, my love.'

'Even when you are kissing and penetrating another girl and not even looking at me, it will still be about us?' she asks doubtfully.

'Yes, because I will be thinking about you watching me. Seeing me with Juliet excited you, do not deny it, and made you desire me even more. Which is why I will let other men, and women, too, use you while I watch and participate, as you will learn to do without letting jealousy get in the way of our shared pleasure.'

Even though her head and her heart have a hard time believing him, her soul knows what he says can be true, if she lets it, and the concept arouses her so much she looks away from him for a moment to gaze around the room.

Everywhere she looks, Isabella sees clothing pushed aside like a curtain to reveal an exquisitely bestial scene… a kneeling man's dark-blond head framed by a sky-blue skirt lifted helpfully out of his way by a lady perched on the edge of a green divan. His dark-gold vest and white shirt framed by her black stockings makes for an arresting combination of colors, but it is the intense concentration of his head embraced by her thighs she finds fascinating, until an urgent motion in the corner of her eye lures her gaze in another direction… this particular lady's dark-red skirt rises like a bloody wave as a man flings it up out of his way and then shoves her thighs apart with cruel impatience, causing her to cry out, either in pain or with pleasure, Isabella cannot be sure which, nor is she certain the lady herself can tell the difference as her pussy is passionately devoured. When her ravenous attacker gets up off the floor and moves around the divan to bend over her, the girl quickly positions her body so her head hangs off the sapphire edge. His huge erection slips neatly between her lips and sinks smoothly down into her throat as he frames his bald bronze skull with her soft white thighs again… but Isabella senses another scenario demanding her attention… Rose and Melody seem to have taken up where they were forced to leave off that morning at breakfast and are devouring Elaine, alternating hungrily between her nipples and her slit as they share her writhing body's unending feast.

'My lord,' she points at Lady Wulvedon's girls, 'please stop them at once. Have Melody chained to the tree and caned, and I want Rose and Elaine forced to kneel in a corner with their hands tied behind their backs so that any man who desires to can make use of their mouths.'

Once again, her wishes are promptly obeyed, and two of Lord Wulvedon's men immediately begin taking advantage of Elaine. They take turns slipping their stiff cocks into her mouth, holding firmly on to her hair so she cannot even think of turning her face away from them. When one hard penis slips out from between her lips, her eyes close in breathless despair as it is instantly replaced by another blood-engorged rod. The men take their time, clearly in no hurry to climax as they cradle their erections lovingly in their gloved hands to feed her, and Isabella senses them relishing the intangible sensation of Elaine's resistance as much as the actual caress of her soft tongue and the contrastingly firm roof of her mouth. But then her attention is drawn back to the principal attraction of Lady Wulvedon's ordeal, when the groans of the men fucking her reach her ears over all the other breathless sounds of pleasure filling the room like the haunted rustling of leaves in a magical forest. Isabella savors the expression of the man on the floor as he comes, running Bridget's pussy swiftly up and down his pulsing cock, and then the other man pulls her face into his groin as he, too, orgasms inside her.

Isabella waits until Bernard's sister is forced to swallow every last drop of semen, and to suffer a final vicious blow of the cane, before she declares, 'Enough. She may go now.'

The instant her mouth is emptied, Lady Wulvedon pushes herself up off the spent man beneath her. Matthew catches her by the arm when she sways on her precarious heels, but she shakes his hand off angrily and walks away, her head held high.

Two of the girls lounging on the cushions quickly get up and follow Bridget out through a dark archway.

Isabella glances at Lord Wulvedon, who is enjoying the spectacle of Melody suffering a riding crop, beneath which her full bottom quivers like pudding. She frowns. 'I said I wanted her caned, my lord.'

'He is merely priming her,' he explains, and at a nod from him, Melody's discomfort becomes a burning misery as the cane slices into her fleshy buttocks, which look especially made for its excruciatingly cutting strokes. She does not hesitate to scream, an amazingly high-pitched sound considering how husky her normal speaking voice is.

Savoring the other girl's increasingly desperate cries, Isabella finishes her wine.

'I have a very special bottle waiting for us in my room.' Lord Wulvedon takes the glass from her and tosses it along with his into the fireplace. 'Come.'

'Yes, master.'

# Epilogue

*An excerpt from the journal of Missa, a direct descendant of Bernard and Isabella Wulvedon:*

I am writing these memoirs even though no words can truly express how much I love my Master. I must admit, I struggled with the term *slave* until I realized it has no more negative connotations than the word *spirit*, which is only a label placed on a force transcending the mind. Some say the spirit is not real and that a slave has no life of her own and both may be true, or not, but that is beside the point. For me to be a slave is to exist in a perpetual state of *love*, also another label for an invisible driving force. By this definition, a slave is not the lowliest creature on earth but rather an elevated being, for it all boils down to how much I love my Master that I am willing to do anything he says. The relationship between a submissive female and a dominant male is so ancient it is practically metaphysical in origin and nature. In the twenty-first century, when faith and marriage have degenerated into empty symbols, the terms *Master* and *slave* possess all the pure power of cosmic hieroglyphs branded into the human psyche with the same fire burning in the heart of the sun, sustaining its beautiful 'slave' the earth. And the moon is just one of the many women and men my Master and I come into sensual contact with, their swinging orbit around us not in the least affecting our profound connection with each other even while hauntingly enhancing it.

Before I met my Master, I went by my baptismal name, Maria Isabel Pita. I still fight depressing battles with her when I am alone, for MIP suffered much emotionally in the hands of men before she met her Master, who named her Missa. Missa is the beautiful phoenix that rose from the ashes of Maria Isabel Pita, who will never be burned again. Missa is everything that was beautiful about MIP, like the pearl freed from its tension-filled shell. Missa is only six months old and as wise and timeless as an ancient priestess serving in the temple of her lord, who she never stopped believing in against all odds. I always knew my Master existed, whether it was in this life or another that we met. Fortunately, it was in this one, and he was the one who christened me Missa, launching me off the page of my fantasies into life and fulfillment. If we're lucky, or if Fate will have it, it will prove to be a long journey. I have no doubt it will be eventful, as it has been already.

He is so sweet and so tender. It never ceases to amaze me that my Master truly loves me. His firmness with me, both physically and emotionally, is the root of my happiness – how deeply he cares for me, as I literally care for him and worship him with my sexual submission. Almost every morning the first thing I do after I wake up is suck my Master's cock. Often my eyes are still closed as I open my mouth and slip his already semi-firm penis between my lips. I break my fast with the sweet milk of his pre-come. Often my mouth is dry, so I lick his shaft a few times to get my saliva flowing, and the way he moans instantly makes my pussy feel deep and warm. Half asleep, I am penetrated by all my dreams of love and happiness in the form of my Master's rigid penis.

When he told me, early on in the beginning of our relationship, going down on him every morning was going to be one of my slave duties, I laughed shyly and thought he was exaggerating. I soon discovered he was not when every morning without fail he gently urged my head down between his legs as we lay naked together in bed. Before I became a slave I always wore panties to sleep, now I rarely ever wear panties at all, and I have to ask permission to do so. I've grown to love the feel of my pussy and my ass beneath dresses, or the short skirts my Master likes me to wear, exposed to the air and the caress of strange surfaces everywhere. Since I began shaving, I am deliciously conscious of my labial lips rubbing against each other as I walk, whether it's in the slick penetrating heat of Miami in the summer, or through the cool caress of an air-conditioned space. There is no longer a barrier woven from conventional thoughts between the world and my sex.

My pussy is never so soft as after my Master fucks it hard. I touch my pubes in wonder they can be so tender and yet so resilient. It's strange, but the more violently my vagina is used the more it can seem to take, and the more it wants to endure. Last Saturday night, after hours in *Plato's*, my cunt was smoldering like the shrine of a burnt out temple, white towels and black lockers vestiges of a more relaxed pagan past and torch-lit catacombs. Yet the next morning on the sea of my Master's waterbed, the unquenchable vessel of my cleft was being rocked towards another cresting, crashing climax for him, and loving it. My clitoris glowed like the full moon at dawn, the intense satisfaction I felt listening to my Master come like the rising sun.

It's hard for me to reach orgasm. My clitoris can be described as eccentric. Like me, it is stubborn and intense. My Master says as my training progresses I will come more easily, and I believe him. Missa is gradually becoming the sensual and relaxed woman MIP always dreamed of embodying. My true nature is blooming beneath my Master's semen. The more I absorb of his being, in every sense, the more desirably erotic I feel and become.

I cannot possibly capture how beautiful my Master is to me with words such as *handsome* or *attractive*, which do not even begin to describe how devastatingly sexy I find him. I can set down a skeleton of details and say he has broad shoulders tapering down to narrow hips and long, strong legs. He is tall, six feet two inches, lean but tender, and his soft brown hair falls almost to his waist. His eyes are an indescribable color somewhere between slate-gray and green, and he has the most beautiful penis I have ever felt and seen. But now I've said too much and nowhere near enough. I will only add he has the most wonderful smile, soft and immutable, as though he is seeing all sorts of fascinating things and possibilities, all within his reach and requiring only a concentrated imagination to grasp and flesh out into reality. His smile, which I feel blessed to look at every day, makes me think of an ancient Etruscan wall painting, so perhaps it's not a coincidence his father's side of the family hails from Etruria, in Italy.

I told my Master last night that sometimes it hurts how much I love him; I don't feel there's enough I can do to show him how much I love him. He says I'm doing a good job, but I know I've only just begun. The only way to truly give myself and everything to him is to put my body at his complete disposal, to do whatever he tells me to and enjoy it without any emotional qualms or effort simply because it is giving him pleasure.

As I write, I am sitting beside the lavender roses he bought me last night, along with chocolate ice cream and a bottle of red wine – a hedonistic holy trinity. And I must confess, my greatest desire is to obey my Master's commands without any reservations getting in the way; without any thoughts of what I think I want, or don't want, damming the inspiring flow of his control. When I think about my Master I get so turned on that just picturing kissing him and fucking him is not enough, and it is not all he wants… so I imagine being bound and restrained from resisting as strangers' dicks penetrate me to multiply the pleasure he takes in possessing me, and I become so excited I wonder why in reality I hesitate to let other men enter me. If pleasing him is all I desire, it should not matter who I have inside me while I do it. It should make no difference to me what form my Master's extended sensuality takes, and truly respecting his judgment in everything should enable me to transcend my own psychologically contrived limits. I am a beautiful woman, and yet how much I enjoyed my own physical attractiveness was eclipsed by perfect superficial images until I met my Master, now I am fully conscious of how powerfully sexy I am. My Master has given me possession of my body as society never did and no other man ever has. I always thought my breasts were not big enough, now I see how lovely they are, with such excitingly big and puffy aureoles, and I love the intensely erotic awareness of my pierced nipples. These are my slave rings and my most treasured possessions because they remind me constantly of the fact that I belong to my Master. My 'great legs' and 'fucking beautiful ass', my long black hair and full lips, my honey-brown 'Egyptian goddess' eyes and the soul behind them, all belong to him now.

THE BEGINNING

# Footnotes

*From *The Metaphysics of Sex* by Julius Evola, English translation 1983 Inner Traditions, New York.

**J.C. Cooper, 1978 Thames & Hudson Ltd., London.

# More exciting titles available from Chimera

All **Chimera** titles are available from your local bookshop or newsagent, or direct from our mail order department. Please send your order with your credit card details, a cheque or postal order (made payable to *Chimera Publishing Ltd*) to: **Chimera Publishing Ltd., Readers' Services, PO Box 152, Waterlooville, Hants, PO8 9FS**. Or call our **24 hour telephone/fax credit card hotline: +44 (0)23 92 783037** (Visa, Mastercard, Switch, JCB and Solo only).

**To order, send:** Title, author, ISBN number and price for each book ordered, your full name and address, cheque or postal order for the total amount, and include the following for postage and packing:

**UK and BFPO:** £1.00 for the first book, and 50p for each additional book to a maximum of £3.50.

**Overseas and Eire:** £2.00 for the first book, £1.00 for the second and 50p for each additional book.

*Titles £5.99. **All others (latest releases) £6.99**

For a copy of our free catalogue please write to:

**Chimera Publishing Ltd**
**Readers' Services**
**PO Box 152**
**Waterlooville**
**Hants**
**PO8 9FS**

or email us at:
**sales@chimerabooks.co.uk**

or purchase from our range of superb titles at:
**www.chimerabooks.co.uk**

**Sales and Distribution in the USA and Canada**

Client Distribution Services, Inc
193 Edwards Drive
Jackson
TN 38301
USA
(800) 343 4499


**Sales and Distribution in Australia**

Dennis Jones & Associates Pty Ltd
19a Michellan Ct
Bayswater
Victoria
Australia 3153

1-800-067.877